WAGON TRAIN CHRISTMAS

LINDA FORD

1

Bent's Fort, 1848

Sophia Lorenzo was about to step from her room on the second level of Bent's Fort when she glimpsed a familiar figure approaching... the wagon master from the wagon train that had recently arrived... a friend of her now-dead husband. She drew back into the shadows of her room, her heart pounding, and waited for the man to pass. She held little Maxie to her shoulder. "Shh. Shh." But her son wanted to go outside to play and he chattered excitedly. At just over a year old, he liked to be on his feet, moving about.

I'm Greta Stern now and Maxie is Cole, she reminded herself. She'd picked the names out of the air, though likely she'd heard them somewhere in the past.

Buck Williams stopped at the sound of Maxie's voice. "Someone sounds happy," he called from outside the room.

Sophia wished she'd thought to close the door but she hadn't expected to see him. Since the arrival a few days ago of the travelers and traders on the wagon train he'd guided from Independence, Missouri, he spent most of his time with the men outside the Fort by the wagon train.

"Yes." She spoke quietly, hoping he would move on. "He's good-natured." At least she was alone in the room that she shared with her wee son so no one would wonder at her strange behavior.

"That's nice." His boots thudded as he continued on by and she remembered to breathe.

She waited, would have retreated to the far corner of her small quarters and stayed there, except Maxie was restless and needed some fresh air.

Clutching her son to her chest, she eased to the door and peeked around the corner. Buck Williams was gone. He must have ducked into the clerk's quarters. Taking in a deep, steadying breath, she left her room and turned the other direction toward the stairs at the end of the line of rooms. The fort had thick adobe walls that she thought offered her protection. But now her fears saw danger in every shadow.

She descended to the courtyard and joined the others, feeling certain Buck would ignore the knot of women.

Her friend Mary Mae, who had recently arrived on the wagon train guided by Buck, welcomed her. "What took you so long, Greta?" Mary Mae knew of the circumstances causing Sophia to use a false name and had promised to respect her reasons, as had her sister, Donna Grace. Sophia couldn't say if their husbands also knew and would likewise keep their silence on the matter. She could only hope and pray it was so.

Sophia did her best to compose her face and keep her voice calm while all the time, her nerves twanged with tension. "Takes a few minutes to collect myself and get Cole organized. He is an expert at squirming." He did just that to prove her words and she set him on his feet. He toddled after the other children on unsteady legs. He'd only learned to walk a few weeks ago, a month before his first birthday, and just before she'd fled Santa Fe.

The women were discussing Christmas activities, but Sophia paid little attention. She had positioned herself so she could keep her eyes on the clerk's room on the upper level.

Buck stepped out and paused to look about. His gaze rested on the women.

Sophia ducked her head, needing to check on Maxie, but even more, needing to keep her face hidden from the man. She did not want him to show the least interest in her.

Sophia turned so she could watch him out of the corner of her eyes.

He descended the steps at the far end and appeared to be headed for the carpenter's shop.

She began to relax and pay attention to what Mary Mae said. "Polly is set on enjoying every Christmas tradition she's ever heard of and I declare she must have asked everyone she knows how they celebrate. She has a very long list." Mary Mae sighed, but Sophia didn't believe for a minute that her friend was put out by the demands of the little girl she and her husband, Warren, had adopted.

Sophia was about to say so when she noticed Buck angling across the open square on a path that would bring him directly toward the women. She looked about, hoping for some excuse to leave, but Maxie played contentedly with Donna Grace's little daughter, Anna, who was only slightly older. He would protest loudly if she snatched him up and hurried away.

Instead, she went to the pair of children and squatted down as if examining what they were doing. From her position she could see Buck's booted feet approach and pause at her side. She kept her face toward the ground as her heart beat frantically. *Please, go away. Please, think you're mistaken in wondering if you recognize me.*

The boots took one step. Then two. "Ladies," Buck said. "Nice to see you enjoying the mild weather."

Mary Mae answered. "I'm hoping it doesn't snow again, but Polly is praying it does."

The others laughed, but Sophia could barely keep balanced on her heels. Her head pounded.

She heard footsteps fading away and allowed herself to shift enough to make sure it was Buck. Yes, thank goodness, he strode off, heading out the wide doors and out of the fort. She could only hope and pray he would go back to the wagons and stay there.

Slowly she straightened and rejoined the others.

Mary Mae gave her a long look. "Do you know him?" she whispered.

"He was a friend of Maximillian's. I'm afraid he will recognize me." She pulled her shawl tighter around her, but it did nothing to stop the chill chasing up and down her body. She lifted the shawl over her head and drew it around her face.

Mary Mae eased her away from the others. "What are you going to do?"

"Hide in my room until he leaves?" Sophia said with a great deal of irony. "I'd be tempted to do exactly that, but Cole—" she must remember to use that name for her son "—would not like it."

"I don't see how you how you can avoid him." Mary Mae looked past Sophia. Sophia spun about fearing Buck had slipped back into the fort without her knowing. She needed eyes in the back of her head to feel safe.

"I must do something. Cole, say goodbye to Anna. We have to go back to our room."

Cole ignored her. He didn't always recognize his new name and she didn't risk calling him Maxie to get his attention. Instead, she squatted down and touched his shoulder. "Tell Anna goodbye."

He stuck out his chin, ready to resist and looking very much like his father. Heaven help her, she couldn't hide his resemblance to Maximillian.

She picked up her little son. "I'm hoping he'll have a nap. All the noise at night has been keeping him awake."

Polly bounced up to her. "But aren't the *posadas* exciting?"

"I like a procession as much as anyone," Sophia admitted. She'd seen many in her years in Santa Fe. "So does Cole." She lifted the boy to her arms.

He threw back his head and arched his back in protest.

She could hardly blame him. It was too early for his customary nap, but she wouldn't be able to relax until she could pull the door closed against any curious stares. Ignoring his whining, she carried him back to their room. The fire in the corner glowed warmly. The dirt floor had been sprinkled to keep the dust down.

She let Maxie run around the room, playing with the tin cup and spoon he favored as toys, while she sank to the thick buffalo robe and collected her thoughts.

The fort was a safe place for now, but she couldn't stay forever. Nor could she avoid Buck forever.

She'd join the first wagon train going west or east. Which wouldn't be anytime soon with winter upon them.

But even if she could escape without Buck discovering her identity, how long could she run and hope to hide?

~

LATER, after Maxie had napped, she put his warm sweater on him and wrapped her shawl about her head, tucking it tight under her chin. It half hid her face and was the only way she could think to disguise herself. She peeked out the door. With no sign of Buck in the square below, she gathered up her courage and went in search of the other ladies. They had gathered at the trade room.

Young Polly examined a selection of knives. "I want to get a gift for Warren."

Donna Grace fingered some calico. "I need to make Elena Rose some new garments. She's growing so fast." Her little daughter had been born on the journey on the Santa Fe Trail.

Sophia let the conversation about making or purchasing Christmas gifts roll over her. She had no money for gifts. Hopefully, Maxie was too young to realize how sparse their celebration would be. A stab of guilt reminded her that she might be causing her son undue hardship, but she couldn't consider the alternative.

The ladies completed their purchases and returned outside to the warm afternoon sun.

Sophia put Maxie down to follow Polly and Anna.

She studied those in the fort, but with so much activity it was hard to keep an eye on everyone. Though she only cared about one person—Buck. Make that two. Her nerves were always twitching with the knowledge that her in-laws would certainly be trying to find her. They wanted to take Maxie from her, having deemed her poverty as reason she didn't deserve to raise him. "He is a Lorenzo and should enjoy all the privileges that name can give him," she'd been informed shortly after she'd laid her husband—Maximillian Lorenzo —to rest.

Maxie saw the fort cat across the square and toddled toward it.

"Watch out," a strident voice called. Several men raced toward the gate. A woman scurried under the protection of the overhanging roof.

Sophia jerked about to see the cause of the commotion. A riderless horse bolted into the enclosed square, head down, snorting and kicking. He continued on at a furious pace.

Her lungs fought for air as she perceived the danger. Where was Maxie? She located her son. Right in the path of the raging animal. He was going to be trampled. She gathered her skirts and raced toward him.

The horse bounded toward Maxie, blinded with its own terror.

Sophia knew her feet moved, she felt the shawl blow from her head. The ground struck at her heels, but it seemed she was frozen, unable to reach her son.

"Maxie," she wailed, her insides ablaze with fear.

The stomping hooves were surely going to reach her son before she could rescue him. They were only inches from striking him.

Arms snatched him from the path of the horse. The animal thundered past, snorting. Spittle spattered her face.

She didn't slow her feet until she reached her son and pulled him from the arms of his rescuer. "Maxie, Maxie," she crooned, holding him tight.

Her legs crumpled and the man caught her.

"Steady now. Take a deep breath."

She did so. Her legs regained their strength and she put several inches between her and the man, embarrassed to have practically collapsed in his arms. When she could force her mouth to work, she looked up at him. "Thank you for—"

She couldn't finish as she stared into Buck's eyes. She swallowed hard as she pulled her shawl back into place. "Thank you for rescuing him." She kept her voice low and her head bent.

"I know you," he said.

She shook her head. "You must be mistaken."

"You called him Maxie."

"It's only a nickname."

Buck bent to look at her son. "He looks like his father."

"I don't see how you can know that." She turned her back to Buck and hurried back to the others.

Mary Mae had observed the situation and pulled her close, hiding her from Buck's view.

Sophia did not need to look his direction to see if he watched her. He knew who she was. Her stomach knotted. Fear clutched at her throat. She tightened the shawl around her face though there seemed little point in trying to hide her identity now.

"I must hide from him," she murmured to Mary Mae.

"I don't see how that is possible," her friend whispered. "Why don't you tell him the truth? He's a good, honorable man. He would understand."

If only Sophia could believe that. But she'd never forget his warning to Maximillian before they'd married. "You could do better. She'll pull you down."

She shuddered. How could she trust a man who shared her in-laws' opinion of her? She couldn't. How was she to avoid him until she could escape?

~

BUCK WATCHED the young woman huddle next to Mary Mae. He had no doubt of who she was—Sophia Morgan. She was the girl whose mother took in boarders. She worked at the home of the Lorenzo family. Last he'd seen of her, his friend Maximillian had decided to marry her.

Buck had advised against it, knowing it was only a form of rebellion on Maximillian's part. Max had always resented the responsibilities his name and position forced upon him.

Upon his arrival at Bent's Fort he'd seen the woman who went by the name of Greta. Buck had been suspicious of her identity. He would have recognized those blue-green eyes anywhere. Her dark blonde hair was the same. Even the challenging expression on her face hadn't changed, and yet he'd doubted himself. Different name. Different place. Was it possible two people looked that much alike?

Hearing her call the little boy Maxie and then seeing the child up close had erased any doubt of who she really was. The boy was practically a mirror image of Maximillian.

Why was she pretending to be someone else, and where was Max?

Somehow he would get to the bottom of this. He owed it to Max for the friendship they shared and how that friendship had pulled Buck from his despair.

It would mean finding her without the others. He left the fort knowing now was not the time. He returned to the wagons he'd guided across the Santa Fe Trail from Independence. The original plan had been to take them to Santa Fe, but winter made crossing the mountains too perilous and things had changed. Sam had died, leaving Polly in Warren's care. Luke and Warren and their new wives had decided to go to California and settle down. Even Gil, his faithful scout, had married and planned to accompany the others west.

Buck wandered past the wagons, greeting the teamsters.

He wasn't sure what his future held. He could likely sign up another bunch of wagons and guide them. He'd been taking his meals with the teamsters, but now told Frenchie he'd be joining the others eating in the dining room of the fort.

"You no like our food?" the big man said.

"There's something I need to take care of."

"There be a lady? Eh?" He laughed.

Buck chuckled. Frenchie would be surprised to know it was because of a lady, but not for the reasons he thought. He bade the man farewell and went further along. A group of Arapaho Indians camped close to the river. He'd had dealings with them before and had become friends with a young couple. He spent a few minutes visiting with them and then, judging it to be time for the evening meal, he made his way back to the fort. If he could time his arrival right, he could enter the dining room after the others were seated, making it impossible for Sophia to avoid him. He might even find a spot close to her.

Inside the fort, the Mexican women prepared meals for their families over the open fire. One looked up as he strode by and smiled.

He ducked into the dining room, inhaled the delicious aromas of roast venison, fresh bread, and something spicy, all with a thick overlay of smoke. St. Vrain and William Bent called to him to join them. He hesitated, saw Sophia crowded in with the other women. Even across the table from them there wasn't enough room for another person, so he waved and accepted the invitation.

"That little girl is determined to make Christmas the best she's ever had," the man to Buck's right said.

Buck guessed they meant young Polly who had been campaigning for a special Christmas since the wagon train left Independence.

"Sounds like a decent idea," another man said.

Buck positioned himself in such a way that he could see Sophia.

She glanced up and their gazes connected across the distance. He saw defiance and something else before she bent to feed the baby.

Buck tried to think what he'd seen. It bothered him to acknowledge it had been fear.

He saw no point in studying the top of her head and shifted his attention to the little one on her knee. The boy was old enough to walk, though his gait was a bit unsteady. He'd put the boy at about a year.

St. Vrain diverted Buck's attention and they discussed the weather.

When Buck looked up again, Sophia was gone. He excused himself and hurried from the table. Mary Mae watched him with a guarded look. She knew something. Would she tell him if he asked? He doubted it.

He stepped from the room and looked about. He didn't see Sophia anywhere. He reasoned she had not had time to reach the second level and escape into her room. He leaned against the nearest upright and prepared to wait. Sooner or later she must leave her hiding place.

His shoulder still rested against the post when the others left the dining room.

The Mexicans, many of the teamsters, and many others joined in a procession that started at the gate and circled the open square with music, singing, and much noise.

Buck shifted his stance so he could watch the spectators. When he saw Sophia slip from the kitchen, he began to slowly make his way in that direction, finding it relatively easy to remain hidden behind the others.

He arrived unnoticed at her side as she looked anxiously to where he had been standing. He leaned close to murmur in her ear. "Why are you pretending to be someone other than Sophia?"

She jolted so violently it was a wonder she didn't drop the little boy from her arms.

He reached for the boy just in case, but Sophia squeezed him tight. Her eyes rounded with fear and she pushed between two brawny men and hurried away.

Determined to get to the bottom of her hiding, he followed at a distance. There were few places for her to go and he could easily overtake her at any time.

She pushed by those watching the procession.

When she reached the gate, he stepped in front of her to stop her leaving the fort.

She looked at him. Even in the last rays of daylight, her eyes flashed like a raging river. "Sir, please let me pass."

He widened his stance to prevent her from getting by him. "Not until you tell me where Maximillian is and why you're hiding."

Her gaze caught his for fraction of a second and then she looked to the adobe wall behind him. "My name is Greta Stern. This is my son Cole. You are mistaken in thinking I am someone else." Her words, delivered in a flat tone, did nothing to convince him.

He caught her arm gently, but in a grasp that she would not easily slip from. "You are Sophia Morgan from Santa Fe. You worked for the Lorenzos and that handsome young fellow is surely son of Maximillian Lorenzo. I demand to know where he is and why you are hiding with his son."

She looked him in the eye, hers flashing anger as brittle as rock. "You demand? By what right do you think you can demand anything of me?" She jerked, trying to free her arm but he had a firm grasp on her. "Let me go before I call for help."

"You could shout your lungs out and no one would hear you above that racket." He tipped his head toward the procession that had grown noisier by the minute.

"So you intend to take advantage of me?"

"Lady, all I want to know is where Maximillian is."

She narrowed her eyes. "He is dead."

His grip loosened and she slipped free, her steps hurried as she returned to the inside of the fort and disappeared in the crowd.

Max was dead? How? When?

Why was Sophia hiding with a boy that looked like Max?

He wanted to know, and only one person could provide those answers.

How was he to persuade her to tell him?

2

Sophia stayed at Mary Mae's side until the procession ended, then begged her to walk with her to her room.

"I still say tell him the truth," Mary Mae said. "He'll understand."

"You know a different Buck Williams than I do. He doesn't approve of me." She told of the conversation she'd overheard between Buck and Maximillian. "He'll want me to take Maxie back to Santa Fe."

"I'm sure if you explain how things are he'll see your side of it."

Sophia shrugged. There was no point in arguing with her friend. Mary Mae and Donna Grace had rich grandparents, and although they had lived simple lives with their mother and father, it wasn't the same as the hand-to-mouth existence Sophia and her mother had known since Sophia's father abandoned them when she was a baby.

Mary Mae must have read Sophia's thoughts. "Not every man is like your father. Some are loyal and trustworthy."

"I guess I'll have to take your word on that. It's certainly not been my experience." She did her best to keep the bitterness out of her voice, but even if she succeeded in keeping her words indifferent, Mary Mae knew Sophia's opinion on the matter.

Mary Mae waited while Sophia tucked Maxie into bed before she asked, "Wasn't your marriage to Maximillian happy?"

Sophia sat back on her heels, trying to decide what to tell her friend. Finally, she let out a long sigh. "It wasn't what I expected. I think he only married me to defy his father and then realized I wasn't what he wanted."

"I'm sorry. I wish—" Mary Mae broke off but her glowing smile said it all.

Sophia rose and hugged her friend. "I'm pleased to see how happy you are with Warren."

"And Polly. She's what brought us together in the first place. Her uncle had died and asked Warren to take her. He needed help caring for her and I was free. I already loved the child so it wasn't a hardship.

And having said that, I better go find her and get her into bed." She hugged Sophia. "I'm sure everything will work out. Remember how we used to pray together?"

Sophia nodded. It seemed a long time ago that she'd felt safe in God's love and care.

Mary Mae took Sophia's hands. "I'm going to pray for you now." She bowed her head.

Sophia did too but she didn't close her eyes. Trust didn't come easily after the things that had happened to her.

"Dear God, our Father in heaven," Mary Mae began. "Help Sophia be able to keep Maxie. Help her to trust Buck so he can help her. And protect us all as You have in the past. Amen."

"Thanks." Sophia felt comforted even if she couldn't hope for the same things Mary Mae did.

Her friend left and Sophia blew out the candle and lay by her son. The flames from the fireplace sent claw-like shadows across the wall. They shifted and moved as if reaching for her. She shuddered. She would never feel safe with Buck knowing who she was. Unlike Mary Mae, she couldn't believe he would want to help her.

Never again would she trust a man… any man. She had to take care of herself and Maxie.

There had to be a way to leave the fort.

~

THE NEXT MORNING, she slipped out the big doors as soon as she'd given Maxie his breakfast. Mary Mae was busy helping Donna Grace with baby Elena and so didn't notice her departure. No one else would care.

She had watched Buck leave earlier and knew he'd gone to the right, toward the river. She went the opposite direction and approached the first group of teamsters.

"Howdy, Miss," a broad-shouldered man called. "Are ye lost?"

She chuckled. "With that adobe castle right there, it would be hard to get lost."

"True. True. Though I'm here to tell you I've seen the snow falling so thick I couldn't see the fort from where I'm sitting this very minute." He rubbed his forehead as if recalling such a day. "Are you out to enjoy the fresh air or is there something I can help you with?"

He appeared to be the spokesman for the others so she addressed her request to him. "I'm needing to travel east. I'm willing to pay passage." She had saved enough gold coins, having sewn them into the inside of her valise for this very purpose.

"Wish we could help you but we're going on to Santa Fe as soon as the mountain pass opens."

"I see. Well, thanks." She started to move on.

"Now then if you ask over there, they might be able to help." He pointed to the nearest circle of wagons.

"Thanks. I'll do that." She walked with purpose, not letting anyone, most of all herself, guess at how ominous a task this was for her.

She saw two men leaning against a wagon wheel, talking, and went up to them. "Would you be departing for Independence soon?"

"No, Ma'am. Waiting to go to Santa Fe. We could take you there."

It was the last place in the world she wanted to go. "Thanks anyway."

Another circle of wagons lay past this one and she made her way toward it.

Luke stepped from between the wagons. "Greta? What are you doing out here?"

Sophia stopped. "I was showing Cole the wagons. I think maybe he's seen enough." She quickly turned back before Luke could ask any more questions.

At the big open gateway, she stepped in just enough to look into the courtyard.

Buck leaned against a post in the far corner, scanning his surroundings.

She drew back, knowing he wouldn't see her in the darkness of the entryway. Knowing he was there gave her an opportunity to go the other direction and seek help. She headed toward the river until she came to the encampment of some Indians. Would they understand English? And even if they did, why would they pick up camp and leave? It didn't seem likely. As she turned to leave, a beautiful native woman in a buckskin dress stood before her.

"Hello," she said.

"Hello. You speak English."

The woman smiled and fluttered her hands to signify she knew a little. "You friend?"

Sophia nodded. "I'm—" She almost said Sophia but even though it seemed wrong to lie to the woman, she said. "I'm Greta." She touched her chest.

"I Niteesh."

They smiled at each other. Niteesh touched Maxie's head. "Baby name?"

"Maxie." She could always explain it as a nickname should anyone question her.

Niteesh called and a little girl ran up to her. "This Lola." There were more syllables than that but Sophia did not understand them.

"You have tea?"

"Yes, thank you." She joined Niteesh around the fire and accepted a cup of strong tea. It was nice to be able to relax and not worry about Buck. Maxie and Lola played together. She guessed Lola to be a little older than her son.

Niteesh waited until Sophia had drained her cup and then she refilled it. "You looking for something."

It was not a question. But Sophia wasn't sure how to answer. She didn't think it likely the woman could offer her any assistance in her desire to get away from the fort.

"Niteesh can help?"

Sophia set her cup aside. "I wish you could."

Niteesh touched the back of Sophia's hand. "Maybe can."

Sophia shrugged. "I'm looking for someone leaving this area. I need to get away."

The woman studied her a few minutes. For some reason, Sophia didn't mind the way Niteesh looked at her, her dark eyes almost mesmerizing.

And then Niteesh nodded. "We leave when time is right. You come with us."

"Thank you. That's very kind. When will the time be right?"

"Only Great Father know."

Sophia wished *she* knew as well. The woman could mean tomorrow, a week from now, or spring. She thanked Niteesh for the tea and rose to leave.

Niteesh followed her as they left the warmth of the fire. "I know white man who will help. I speak to him."

"Thank you." Again, Sophia didn't know if Niteesh meant she'd ask in the near future or some distant date, but it gave her an excuse to return and escape the tension she felt in the fort. "Can I come back to see what you've learned?"

"You come any time. I speak to man tonight."

Finally a ray of hope. Someone willing to help her.

"I'll be back." Reluctantly she returned to the fort, pausing outside the gate to look around for Buck. She didn't see him and proceeded to the interior where she again paused to search her surroundings. She didn't see him, but rather than ease her tension, it made her nerves twitch.

She'd sooner know where he was and be able to stay out of his way than be constantly watching for him, fearing she would accidently cross his path.

∾

BUCK HAD WATCHED for Sophia all morning, determined to get the truth from her. Somehow she'd managed to keep out of sight. Could she be holed up in her room? Well, sooner or later she'd have to come out and when she did, he would be waiting.

Except he couldn't hang about waiting. Curling his fists in frustration, he went out to the wagons. Luke looked up at his approach. "Had a visitor this morning," he said. "That Greta woman with her little boy."

Buck ground to a stop. Sophia? No wonder he hadn't been able to discover her whereabouts in the fort. "She was here? What did she want?"

"Said she was showing the little guy the wagons. Saw her talking to the men over there." Luke turned back to adjusting the canvas.

Buck stared at the other camps. What was she up to? He strode toward the first circle and asked.

"She was wanting passage to Independence. Told her we was headed for Santa Fe as soon as we could travel over the mountains. She wasn't interested. Kind of got the feeling she wanted to leave soon. Didn't tell her that no one will be leaving until the weather changes." The man glanced at the sky. "It don't feel right to me."

Buck looked to the sky as well. Although it was clear, a mist hung over Pike's Peak in the distance. A harbinger of change. He thanked the man and returned to the wagons he was in charge of.

Luke eyed him but his expression changed as Buck drew closer, and Buck wondered how much he knew about Sophia. How much did Donna Grace and Mary Mae know? Had they been acquainted back in Santa Fe? But he didn't ask, knowing Luke would keep his own counsel on the matter.

Buck would find out the truth from Sophia herself.

He tended to camp chores, made a few comments about repairs needed on some of the wagons, and joined the teamsters for the noon meal. He knew Sophia and her little son retired to their room after they'd eaten so he didn't hurry back to the fort. Instead, he inspected the oxen and mules belonging to his wagon train.

Only then did he enter through the big gate and lower himself to a narrow wooden bench under the shelter of the portico. He stretched his legs out, then thought better of it, knowing the sight of his booted feet would give away his presence, so he drew his legs up. From where he sat, he could see the door to Sophia's room, hoped she couldn't see him, and he waited.

His legs cramped and he shifted position. He stretched his neck and readjust his hat.

And he waited. How long did the little boy nap?

Around him murmured the customary blend of

voices in several languages. He heard French, Spanish, English, and a smattering of German. Smoke from the many fires drifted through the air and the smell of food came from the kitchen.

Mary Mae and her sister crossed the courtyard toward the trade room. Mary Mae noticed Buck and broke her stride. She looked ready to head his direction and then fell into step with her sister again.

Buck leaned over his knees and returned his attention to the upper level and the closed door of Sophia's room.

A few minutes later his patience was rewarded. The door cracked open. A pause as if she looked through the narrow opening.

He pressed back into the protection of the roof and waited.

The door slowly opened wider. Sophia poked her head out and looked to the right and left. Her gaze swung across the courtyard and swept along the covered walkway, pausing to give every group of people study. Then she stepped out, the little boy in her arms, pulled the door closed, and hurried toward the stairs.

He unfolded from his position and made his way along the walkway, sticking close to the wall, hoping she wouldn't notice his approach. At the end of the portico, he stopped, biding his time till just the right moment.

She reached the ground and started toward the trade room.

He strode from his place and met her face to face.

She glanced about as if hoping for escape.

Several of the Mexican woman watched them, no doubt curious as to why he'd stopped her.

Buck eased back on his heels, his arms akimbo. "We need to talk."

Sophia rocked her head back and forth and sent desperate looks toward the trade room but none of her friends came to the rescue.

"I want to know what happened to Maximillian." He kept his voice low, hoping not to attract attention from any of those in the courtyard.

"He died."

"I'm sorry for your loss. He was a friend of mine."

Something flared in her blue-green eyes, but it fled before he could identify it.

"Was it an accident? Illness?" He persisted, though he couldn't say why he pressed for details except to try to learn why she was pretending to be someone other than Sophia Morgan, and why she had a son who looked so much like Maximillian that the baby must surely be his friend's son. "Did he marry you?" He hoped Maximillian had had the decency to give his son a name.

Sophia drew the baby to her shoulder, hiding his face against her shawl. "Against your advice, he did marry me." She pushed past him and hurried to the trade room.

He didn't follow. Against his advice? What was she talking about? More questions formed than had been answered, but he'd not learn anything more from her while she was with the other women, so he strode from the fort.

Maximillian was dead but Buck didn't know how or when.

He and Sophia had married and had a son.

Why was Sophia running and hiding? Didn't the boy belong with family back in Santa Fe? The Lorenzos were well able to take care of Sophia and little Maxie.

He would not call the boy Cole no matter what Sophia said.

And when had he ever told Maximillian he shouldn't marry Sophia? He tried to recall the events of almost two years ago when he'd last seen his friend. Then he remembered the conversation Sophia must have overheard. He must explain it to her and make her understand.

He turned on his heel and returned to the fort where he leaned against the wall next to the door to the trading room.

The women conducted their business and stepped into the winter sunshine.

It suited his purposes rather well that Sophia, with Maxie in her arms, followed several steps behind the others.

He fell in at her side, ignoring the way her eyes burned with warning to stay away.

"Please give me a chance to explain."

She shifted Maxie so he was on her other side. Buck knew it was so the boy was further from him. "What's to explain? You didn't think I was good enough for Maximillian and made that clear to him."

"That's not how it was."

Sophia stopped and faced him. "I was well aware of the fact that I was below him in station. He was rich. I was poor. His parents didn't approve. My mother didn't approve."

"That's what I was trying to make him understand."

She turned away but he had to finish and caught her elbow. The look she gave him was enough to leave scorch marks on his face.

"I thought he only wanted to marry you to defy

his parents. That's why I told him he shouldn't do it. And you were so young. Only seventeen." Maximillian was the same age as Buck, twenty-three at the time. But a very worldly-wise twenty-three while Sophia had been so young and innocent, a flower not yet in full bloom.

Her gaze returned to him and held his like a vise. "I guess you can explain it any way you like. It changes nothing."

"Except it should. As his friend, I'd like to help you, but first, I need to know what's going on that you are here, pretending to be someone you're not."

He wouldn't have thought her gaze could burn hotter, but it did. But years of standing his ground before angry men and other challenges allowed him to meet her look without showing a smidgen of being ill at ease.

"If you care about Max and his son, you will call me Greta and him Cole, and you'll pretend you don't know me." She marched away.

He stared after her, too stunned to move.

Why was she so determined to pretend she wasn't Maximillian's widow and Maxie his son?

3

Sophia had to get away. Buck's persistence and his knowledge of her true identity meant she could no longer feel safe at the fort. Perhaps she could pay someone to take her to one of the small outposts. Or maybe one of the Indian tribes would let her live with them.

Niteesh had said she'd speak to a man, and Sophia hurried through supper, grateful that Buck did not come to the dining room. She knew her reprieve was temporary. He was a man used to having people do as he requested. Mary Mae had spoken highly of his control on the wagon train journey to the fort.

Being in charge of those in his care was one thing.

Wanting to know about her life with Maximillian and his family was something else entirely.

She told Mary Mae of Niteesh's invitation to
visit and as soon as she could, she slipped from the
fort. The music and dancing of the Mexicans made
it easy to leave without being noticed. Outside the
fort, she drew her warm shawl around herself and
Maxie. The nights tended to be cold. They'd had
snow a few days ago but, it had vanished except for
well-shaded spots.

The warm firelight of Niteesh's camp guided
Sophia to her new-found friend.

"Greta, you come." Niteesh drew her to the
warmth of the fire and gave her a cup of hot,
strong tea.

Sophia wondered if Niteesh had a husband, but
the sound of deep voices within the tent made her
think he was inside. She was anxious to discuss the
matter closest to her heart but didn't want to be
rude, so they talked about the weather and the children for a few minutes; then Niteesh set aside
her cup.

"I speak to man as I tell you."

The weight that had burdened her shoulders for
the past few days lightened. "Did he offer to help?"
Sophia looked about but saw no one. Her heart
sank, even though she knew it was foolish to think

they could leave right away. No one traveled at night, especially with a young child.

"He will say for himself."

Niteesh rose and waved forward a man from the inside of her tent.

"No." The word erupted from Sophia's mouth as Buck stepped into the circle of light.

"I take baby. You talk." Niteesh guided Lola and Maxie inside the tent making it impossible for Sophia to grab her child and run.

She sank back to the ground where she'd been seated, stiffened her shoulders, and clamped her lips together.

He sat a few feet from her, his legs crossed. Although they were a goodly distance apart she felt crowded by his presence.

Neither spoke. She determined she would not be the first to break the silence. She had nothing more to say to this man.

He cleared his throat.

Did he think she would feel compelled to respond? She didn't.

He shifted about and leaned over his legs more, bringing his face closer to her.

She stared at the flames wishing they would leap up, perhaps send out sparks that would force him to move away. But no, the fire burned steadily. She allowed the faintest sigh.

A log snapped in the fire, causing her nerves to tense.

If not for Maxie needing her, she'd be tempted to run into the darkness and hide among the bushes.

Finally, he spoke, his voice so soft his words were almost lost in the crackle of the flames. "I just want to know what happened."

She had promised herself she would keep silent, but his continual demand to know more irritated her. "Why? What difference does it make to you or anyone else?" She clamped her teeth together to stop the torrent of words that threatened to pour forth.

"A few years back I was in a bad state." His voice was low forcing her to concentrate on his words. "I doubt you know this about me. Few do. But I was married."

Sophia watched him as he talked. He stared beyond the flames, his gaze going into his past. Suddenly she was as full of questions about him as he was about her. But she waited, letting him decide how much he cared to tell her.

"We had set out for Oregon on a wagon train, but Edie was far too adventuresome. Or maybe it was independent. She didn't always listen to advice.

And it got her into trouble." His voice deepened and Sophia knew without him saying anything more that his wife's independence had caused something bad to happen.

"She'd been warned not to wander from camp, but she saw some early berries and wanted to enjoy them. She didn't tell anyone or ask me to go with her." He drew in a breath that went on several seconds. "Bears also wanted the berries, and she clashed with one."

Sophia gasped.

He nodded. "The bear tore her so badly she only survived a few hours." He shuddered. "It was a slow gruesome death for her."

His pain palpated through her and, despite her wish to keep her distance both physically and emotionally, she could not withhold comfort and she shifted marginally closer. Close enough she could reach out and squeezed his forearm.

"I'm so sorry for your loss and what you endured."

He nodded, still gazing into the distance. "I blamed myself for not taking better care of her. I blamed her for not listening to advice." A beat of heavy silence, and then a slow drawing in of air. "I left the Oregon Trail and joined wagons on the Santa Fe Trail. I helped the wagon master and learned a lot, but then one day in Santa Fe, I hit bottom and couldn't think of any reason to keep on."

Sophia tried to imagine a discouraged, defeated Buck, but couldn't do so.

Buck's soft chuckle made her lean closer to look into his face. Why was he laughing?

He turned to meet her gaze. "As I sat and felt sorry for myself, Maximillian came by. He was happy and laughing, telling everyone he met that he had just bought the fastest horse in all of Mexico and beyond, and would challenge anyone to a race. He was so eager to try his horse that he offered fifty dollars to anyone who would race him. He had quite a few takers, then he saw me. I was leaning against a post doing nothing much and he strode up to me. 'Mister, join the fun.' I said I wasn't interested, but he wouldn't take no for an answer. So I raced him. Didn't win, but by the time the race was over with Maximillian crowing over his win, I'd forgotten my dark thoughts." Buck chuckled again. "He had a way of enjoying life."

Sophia nodded. "I know."

Buck's gaze held hers, deep calling to deep; the shared joy of knowing Maximillian forging a bond.

"He invited me to join him for supper. By the time the wagon train was ready to leave, I was a different man. Maximillian made me see that life was to be enjoyed. But respected."

Sophia stared into the fire. The logs were burning down and the coals danced like they were alive. "That's what he did for me too." At first. Then things changed. But she wouldn't tell Buck that. Let him remember the happy-go-lucky Maximillian. The one upon whom his parents had once doted.

Buck shifted so he could look directly at her. "I owe Maximillian for his friendship and what it meant to me. That's why I want to help you. I know he would want me to."

The gentleness in Buck's voice called to Sophia's heart, but she steeled herself against it. She must think of Maxie and his safety. She reached for the fire as if to warm herself but really, it was to twist away from Buck.

"Sophia, who are you running from and why? Let me help you. For Maximillian's sake. For his memory."

Buck almost convinced her. She'd shared some sweet times with Maximillian to begin with.

"His son should be back in Santa Fe where the Lorenzos are. Where he will be safe and well cared for."

She bounded to her feet.

He blinked then rose, watching her with wariness.

She leaned closer, her eyes burning with indignation and defense. "He is safe and well cared for now. With me. Just leave us alone." She needed to push by him to get to the tent for Maxie, but she hesitated to do so.

"I didn't mean it that way, but he is Max's son and heir. Isn't that important to you?"

"It means nothing to me. Riches do not mean anything. He is my son and I will take care of him." She put out her arm to push past him.

She managed to thank Niteesh for her hospitality though her mouth felt like she'd swallowed half a buffalo robe.

"Man help you?" Niteesh asked.

"He tried." It was the best answer she could give. She thanked the woman again then hurried out with Maxie.

"Let me carry the boy for you."

It seemed it was too much to hope Buck would leave her in peace.

She turned her back, but Buck held out his arms and Maxie crowed with delight to have a man carry him. Reluctantly she let Buck take him. Which meant she must walk beside him back to the fort.

Light came from the moon and a nearby campfire, but she had to walk carefully on the uneven ground to keep from stumbling. Buck seemed to realize it and slowed.

As they neared the gate, six riders approached the fort. The man guarding the gate asked them to identify themselves.

"Name's Bart Johnson and this is my crew. We've come over the Raton Pass from Santa Fe. Mighty glad to reach this place."

Sophia's feet froze to the ground and she couldn't move. Who would be coming from Santa Fe and why? She could think of only one answer. The Lorenzos had figured out where she'd gone and sent someone after her.

Buck realized she no longer followed at his side and turned. "Is something wrong?"

Her mouth refused to work and she couldn't answer.

Buck leaned closer so he could see her face. "You look scared. Why?"

Still she couldn't answer.

He shifted Maxie to one side and Sophia saw her son had fallen asleep in Buck's arms. For a quick heartbeat she envied Maxie his place of security. Would she ever live without a shadow of fear clinging to her?

Buck caught her arm and drew her to his side. "You're safe. I won't let any harm come to you."

His assurance loosened her tongue. "You don't know what you're saying."

"Sophia, why won't you trust me and let me help you?"

Trust him? It was tempting. "I can't. You think I should go back to Santa Fe."

He studied her. "Perhaps I would think differently if you explained why you're so afraid."

Maxie snuffled in his sleep reminding Sophia she needed to get him to his bed. And the safety of her room.

Only how safe would she be if the newcomers had been sent by the Lorenzo family? She couldn't stay in her room until someone decided to leave the fort in the direction of Independence. She reached for Maxie.

Buck shook his head. "I'll carry him. I don't mind."

She forced her feet to move forward.

Buck stayed at her side, often glancing down at her.

They reached the gate. Her heart thudded so hard she wondered why Buck didn't hear it. She couldn't stay here, not knowing when someone would appear and perhaps snatch Maxie away.

She'd found no way of leaving. She couldn't strike out on her own, and no one was prepared to take her.

Would Buck help her because of his friendship with Maximillian?

Dare she risk everything based on that friendship?

~

BUCK COULD FEEL the fear in Sophia. She moved with a woodenness that made her almost stumble. Her breath came in little puffs that had nothing to do with the chill in the air. Something about the newcomers had sent her into a panic.

At the gate she stopped as if her feet had grown to the ground.

He halted as well and waited for her to move.

She backed away. "Can we talk?"

"Now?" He'd asked her the same question on more than one occasion and each time she'd refused. "Here?" The evening was deepening and the boy slept in his arms. He had to admit he liked the feel of a child's head resting in the hollow of his shoulder. There was a time he had hoped to enjoy the experience with children of his own. That dream had died along with Edie. After that, he had closed his heart to the possibility, not wanting to risk the pain of loving and losing nor the guilt of failing to protect the one he loved.

He pulled his thoughts together and looked about. The teamsters at his wagon train were huddled about a fire, with Pete playing his harmonica. "Come with me." Luke would not object to his taking Sophia to one of his wagons. They could talk there without being overheard. He led the way, half expecting Sophia to object and refuse to accompany him, but she followed readily enough.

At the back of the wagon he held out his free hand to help her climb into the back, then got in with little Maxie still sleeping in his arms. "He sleeps soundly, doesn't he?" he commented as he seated himself on the wagon floor.

"I can take him." Sophia reached out for her son.

"No need to disturb him." Though he wondered what it would take to waken the boy.

She settled back against the side of the wagon. "You and Maximillian were friends."

He saw no need to respond as she knew the answer.

"May I presume upon that friendship?" She sat facing the fire and the shadows of the flames through the canvas filled her face with hard plans. He heard the uncertainty in her voice.

"I want to help in any way I can."

She nodded, swallowed hard, and rubbed her lips together before she spoke again, slowly and so softly he leaned closer to hear her. "I need someone to take me to Independence right away. Will you?"

He sat back, too surprised to answer.

"I must go right away."

"What is so urgent that you want to set out in bad weather with a baby and, I presume, without the protection of a full wagon train?" The logistics of it and the extent of the risks appalled him. Before he would point those out he wanted to hear her explanation.

"I don't expect you to understand my reasons."

"I'm afraid I must know them before I would contemplate such a journey."

She pulled her feet under her and prepared to stand.

He caught her arm, remembering how her touch back at the tent of his Indian friends had helped ease the pain of his memories of Edie. Could he hope his hand on her arm would do the same and make her tell him what was really going on? "Sophia, if we're to travel together, trust will be absolutely essential. Why not start now?"

She settled back down and looked at his hand on

her arm but did not shake it off. He left it there, feeling that somehow he offered protection.

"Very well, I don't expect you to believe me, but I'll tell you what I am afraid of." Her voice grew hoarse. "Maximillian's parents want to take Maxie from me and raise him to be a proper Lorenzo. They don't want me in the picture. They don't think I am a fit parent."

He could understand why they wanted their grandson, but to take him from Sophia seemed harsh. "Are you sure you're not mistaken?"

She shook off his hand. "I knew you wouldn't believe me. Forget it."

"They doted on Maximillian. Why wouldn't they welcome both you and Maxie with open arms?"

Her scowl was exaggerated in the harsh light of the fire. "You said it yourself. Max could do better than marry a poor servant girl like me."

"I didn't mean for you to hear me." Somehow he knew that wouldn't soothe her. "I simply thought he was doing it for all the wrong reasons and you'd both end up hurt."

"Congratulations. Turns out you were right."

He felt nothing but sorrow at her words. At the tremor in her voice, he wished he could comfort her in some way. He shifted around so they were shoulder to shoulder. "I am sorry. What happened?"

She shuddered. "Maximillian's parents disowned him. We were forced to live in a tiny house. I didn't mind. I was used to living poorly but Maximillian resented it, and he soon grew to resent me for being the cause." Her voice quivered.

Buck's heart squeezed at the sound. He slipped an arm about her shoulders, surprised when she didn't resist. Here he sat, the man who meant to spend his life guarding his heart, holding a woman in one arm and a baby in the other. And it felt just right. Of course, it was only temporary so he didn't have to worry about the risks of the position he was in.

"Maximillian started drinking."

Buck closed his eyes against the knowledge of what that meant. He'd seen how mean Max could get. "Did he hurt you?"

She shrugged. "There are many ways to be hurt."

"True enough." His arm tightened about her and she leaned against him. Something inside him warmed as if the flames had leapt through the canvas and landed in his chest. He wanted to make things right for Sophia and her son. "He provided for you, didn't he?"

"He wouldn't get real work. His job, he said, was to run the Lorenzo ranch."

"How did you survive?" He was almost afraid to ask.

"Mama made sure we had food. Other than that, I survived as I always have. But don't worry, I can pay for passage. Maximillian had gambled and won a small stash of gold, and I inherited it after he died."

"How did he die?"

"Got beat up. I expect it had something to do with his gambling habits. His family allowed him to be buried in the family plot but didn't attend the funeral. And then—" she shivered so hard her teeth rattled. "His uncle Gilberto came to the door demanding I turn Maxie over to him so he could be raised as a Lorenzo should be. He said my baby would get the best of care and would never know of his mother and her unsuitability."

"Oh, Sophia. That's so wrong. What did you do?"

"I slammed the door in his face and barred it. He banged and threatened. Then said he would be back with help. I grabbed Maxie and a few things and fled. I couldn't go to my mother. That would be the first place they'd look. I saw a wagon train about to depart and paid one of the teamsters to let me ride in his wagon."

"You got this far. Why didn't you go the rest of the way with him?"

She snorted. "He learned who I was and refused

to have anything more to do with me." She turned her face up to him. "Do you believe me?"

"I do." He knew enough about the Lorenzos to know they would stoop to such behavior. It was their rigid control that Maximillian had rebelled against.

"So you'll help me get away?"

He considered how to answer without giving her cause to think he wouldn't do it. "You think those recent arrivals might be sent by the Lorenzos?"

"I fear it."

"Why don't you let me find out before we take any action? If they aren't a threat to you then there is no need to rush away ill prepared, with winter weather upon us."

She straightened, allowing cold air to hit his chest. "I will never be safe from them."

"I will take care of you." He wanted to think it was for Maximillian's sake and the friendship they'd enjoyed. But the truth was, Sophia and Maxie needed him, and it provided a chance to prove he could protect someone in his care. A chance to make up for how he'd been unable to do so with Edie. "I promise I will keep both you and Maxie safe."

The flames leapt as if someone had thrown another log on the fire, and in the flare of light he was able to see her expression go from hopeful to guarded.

"That's a mighty big promise. What happens if you fail?"

"I don't plan to fail."

She chuckled softly. "Not too many of us plan it. It just sneaks up and takes us by surprise."

"Nevertheless, if you let me, I will do everything I can to keep you and Maxie safe."

She tipped her head back. "The Lorenzos are a powerful family."

"Only in Santa Fe." It wasn't totally true, but their power weakened as the distance grew. "Sophia, trust me."

She shifted so she sat looking directly into his face.

He met her gaze steadily, letting her search deep, hoping she would see how much he wanted to help and how much it mattered to him. As he'd told her, he owed Maximillian for making him remember how much joy life had to offer. Now he wanted to do the same for Max's widow. And ultimately, his child.

When she finally nodded and her eyes filled with resolve, he felt as if he had won a prize.

"Very well, I will trust you, Buck Williams. I

hope you don't live to regret being involved in my life."

He smiled at the mix of relief and warning in her eyes. "I won't regret anything." He could not explain why he made such a broad statement nor why he meant it so thoroughly.

Little Maxie arched his back and rearranged himself.

"He needs to go to bed," Sophia said with some reluctance, Buck thought, knowing it was likely due to the fact she didn't want to go to the fort and perhaps encounter someone sent by the Lorenzos.

But a warm room awaited her and her son back there. He would ensure they also were safe.

"I'll take you to the fort and escort you to your room."

She nodded. "I would hide there if I could."

"No need. I'll see who the newcomers are. If they are from the Lorenzos, I will speak to them. So long as you are with me, no harm can befall you." It was almost like the promise he'd given Edie, but she'd chosen to go her own way. Sophia was free to do what she wanted as well. "I can only promise to keep you safe if we stay together." He knew he couldn't follow her everywhere, nor could she accompany him at all times. "If I can't be with you, I will make sure someone else is guarding you." Big

Frenchie was his first choice. The man was a gentle giant but no one would dare challenge him.

"Very well. Let's do what we have to do."

He eased from the wagon and helped her down.

They walked side by side back to the fort. As they passed through the entranceway, she pressed closer to his side. He kept her to his right so his body blocked her from view. They climbed the steps to the upper level. He paused at the door to her room. By rights, he shouldn't enter.

She understood his hesitation, took Maxie from his arms, and lay him on his back on the buffalo robe. He snuffled once, threw his arms above his head, and slept.

Sophia covered him, then joined Buck at the doorway. "He's a very sound sleeper." She looked up at Buck. "Thank you for believing me and for offering to help."

He squeezed her shoulder. "Stay here in the morning until I come for you."

Her gaze searched his as if wanting to assure herself she could trust him. After a moment in which he didn't dare blink, she nodded.

"I'll wait for you."

He paused, wanting more, but he couldn't even say what he wanted. He let his gaze roam over her face and linger on her lips. Then he shook himself.

"Good night then." He backed from the room and closed the door.

"Good night," she called softly.

He went in search of the newcomers. He must learn who they were and what brought them to the fort this time of year.

And if they were from the Lorenzos, what would he do?

4

S ophia had been awake a long time before she heard the first sounds of the fort coming to life. The Mexican ladies could be heard preparing breakfast for their families. A man called to the animals in the corral and a mule brayed. Fresh smoke filled the air. She'd slept very little as her emotions ricocheted from one extreme to another. She'd decided to tell Buck what happened between her and Maximillian. And he believed her! She almost laughed aloud into the darkness. Instead, she let relief flood her with joy. Believing her was almost as good as saying she was a good mother, a worthy woman. *Wait. Don't start building castles out of dreams.* She'd learned the risk of wanting something so badly that she ignored the warning signs. She'd known Maximillian's parents didn't approve of her. Her own mother had said Max only saw her as someone different than his usual friends. And if she would allow herself to confess it, Buck had spoken out because he'd seen the risks of a marriage between two such unlikely people.

It wasn't because of their different stations in life that they weren't happy as a married couple, she admitted. It was because their reasons for agreeing to marry weren't valid. Like Buck said, Maximillian only wanted to defy his parents and exert some independence. And she was so flattered by the attention of a Lorenzo man that she didn't allow herself to see past that.

She would not make the mistake again. And now with Maxie to consider, she didn't consider another marriage a possibility. It would take more trust than she was capable of to think another man would love her son like his own. Her emotions fell to the bottom of the arc. Her own father had taught her about the difficulty of loving a child. He couldn't even love his own flesh and blood enough to stick around.

No, she cautioned herself. It was enough to rely on Buck to protect her from the Lorenzos. All she would ask or accept from him was escape from Maximillian's family.

Her traitorous feelings reminded her of how safe and valued she felt in the shelter of his arms as they sat in the wagon discussing her life with Maximillian. When was the last time a man had held her to offer comfort and protection?

The answer was painfully simple.

Never.

Maximillian had been demanding from their first meeting, wanting her to allow him liberties that she couldn't give him. Perhaps that had been part of his desire to marry her. Simply to conquer her.

In the darkness of her room, she made herself another promise. She would never again let a man conquer her.

Maxie stirred and she rose and prepared for the morning. Maxie went to the door and fussed, wanting to get out to eat and run.

"We must wait," she soothed. Even if she hadn't given her promise to Buck, she had no desire to venture out and run the chance of encountering the newcomers.

The sound of approaching footsteps sent a trickle of fear through her. What was to stop anyone from coming? The wooden slab between her and the rest of the fort provided minimal protection, though all she had to do was scream and a dozen people would race to her rescue. That is if she could make her voice work, for her throat had closed off. She grabbed Maxie and retreated to the far corner of the room.

The footsteps thudded to her door and stopped. Knuckles rapped.

"It's me."

She recognized Buck's voice. Relief left her weak. She set Maxie on the floor and hurried to open the door.

Buck had removed his hat. His thick brown hair had been brushed back. His brown eyes watched her intently and smiled even before his mouth curved.

He had, she realized, the kind of strong face that made it almost easy to trust him.

"You'll be relieved to know that those men that arrived yesterday are old trappers. They've come to replenish supplies, but I think they really came because they realized it's almost Christmas and wanted to celebrate."

Sophia hadn't realized how heavy her worries had become until he made his announcement and her hands came up of their own accord as if freed from a weighty burden. She grabbed his arms and could barely restrain herself from hugging him.

"I'm so glad to hear that." She turned to call

Maxie forward but the boy was already at her knees. He pushed against Buck's legs.

"Up."

Sophia knew that's what Maxie had said but didn't know if Buck would recognize the word.

"It's up you want, is it?" He lifted Maxie and swung him into the air earning him a belly laugh.

If Sophia wasn't so intent on never again giving her heart to a man, she would have fallen in love with Buck right then and there as he settled Maxie in the crook of his arm and the two grinned at each other.

Buck didn't even seem to mind that Maxie drooled over his hand. He turned to Sophia. "Shall we go to breakfast?" He offered her his arm and she rested her hand on it.

She ignored the question ringing in the back of her mind. Why was she acting like this was more than him protecting her?

As soon as they reached the ground, she stepped away. She would have taken Maxie too, but her son had eyes for no one but the big man grinning at him.

Mary Mae watched them approach. Her eyebrows reached for her hairline.

Sophia knew her friend would demand all the details of what had changed. As they reached the dining room, she took a protesting Maxie from Buck.

"Come along, Cole," she murmured, sending Buck a look she hoped informed him he must continue to call her Greta and Maxie, Cole, as long as they were with others.

He nodded in understanding. His eyes darkened and his mouth turned up into a crooked grin.

She wondered what it meant until he patted Maxie on the back. It seemed he enjoyed spending time with her son.

"See you later, little guy."

Maxie gurgled his pleasure.

She hurried to join the others, crowding in between Mary Mae and Donna Grace.

Mary Mae leaned close to whisper in Sophia's ear. "I told you he could be trusted."

Sophia whispered back. "That remains to be seen, doesn't it?"

"Oh, you are such a doubter."

Sophia shrugged. Her words were a good reminder to herself. She could expect only so much from Buck, and best if she remembered that.

She promised herself she wouldn't look for him at the table across from where she sat, but she did anyway, and her gaze met his. At the way he looked at her—his eyes full of promise, and something more, that was surely only in her own wayward mind—her heart kicked so hard against her ribs she almost called out.

Afraid her friends would notice, she ducked her head and stared at the food on her plate, though it could have been unbaked beans for all the notice she took of it.

She barely realized when the meal was over. Only after Buck strode from the room did she see that her plate was empty, Maxie had somehow been fed and Mary Mae waited at her side.

Sophia rose and headed for the door. Mary Mae stayed right with her and managed to shepherd her to a bench in a quiet corner.

"Now tell me what happened!"

"Nothing really. Those strangers rode in last night as I was returning to the fort and I feared the Lorenzos might have sent them. You told me to trust Buck so I told him why I was hiding. He said he would make sure no harm came to Maxie."

"Or you, I assume."

Sophia shrugged, hoping her warm cheeks didn't reveal the truth. "I guess so."

Mary Mae squealed. "I'm so happy for you."

Sophia composed her face then turned to her friend. "You're happy that I live in fear of someone taking Maxie?"

Mary Mae sobered. "Of course not." She grinned. "But you and Buck—" She hugged herself and looked so happy that Sophia had to laugh.

"You can stop being so pleased. There is no such thing as me and Buck."

Mary Mae tilted her head and looked superior. "That's what I said about me and Warren and now look at us."

Sophia looked about. "Where is Warren?" A sure-fire way to divert Mary Mae from her current topic.

Mary Mae sighed. "He's repairing wagons for our journey over the mountains." She laughed. "Imagine, we—along with Luke and Donna Grace, and Gil and Judith—are going to start afresh in California." Her eyes narrowed and she studied Sophia. "Are you coming with us?"

Her friend had suggested before that Sophia go west with them. She had seriously considered it, thinking it would provide the best escape. If the Lorenzos didn't find her before then. "I might just do that if everyone approves of me going."

"No reason they wouldn't. Especially if Buck comes along."

"Please don't be linking my name with Buck's like that." She closed her eyes against the flash of a dream she'd had since she was a child. In her dream she lived with a man who loved and adored her and who would never leave her. She remembered how she imagined being swept off her feet in a welcoming embrace when the man returned home. The man had never had a face she could recall but her body knew the strength of those arms and the warmth in her heart.

With a jolt she saw the man now and he had Buck's face. It couldn't be. Her imagination was running wild.

She sprang to her feet. "I have something to do."

Mary Mae called after her as Sophia hurried from the fort and turned right. Not until she saw Niteesh's tent did she realize that was her destination.

Niteesh seemed to be waiting for her and caught her hand to draw her toward the fire. She waited for Sophia to get seated.

"You talk to Buck?"

Sophia nodded, too confused to talk.

Niteesh seemed to understand and prepared tea and handed Sophia a cup while Maxie and Lola played to one side.

"Buck is good man," Niteesh said after a lengthy silence.

Again Sophia nodded. Her heart was so full of confusion she couldn't begin to sort it out.

Niteesh touched Sophia's knee. "You are worried."

"I want to make Maxie a new shirt." She almost laughed at her own words. Where had that thought come from, and yet, as soon as she spoke, she knew it was what she needed to do.

The rest of her thoughts could drift away.

"Wait here." Niteesh pushed to her feet, went into the tent, and emerged with a doeskin so soft Sophia pressed it to her cheek. Tears welled up for no reason other than the doeskin was like a gentle caress.

She shook her head. She did not need a gentle caress nor did she long for one.

"You make shirt. I show you."

Sophia was about to refuse when she saw the look in Niteesh's eyes. The woman was not simply offering a beautiful piece of leather, but her friend-ship. "Thank you. It's the loveliest thing I've ever had."

Niteesh showed her how to cut the skin into pieces the right size.

Sophia discovered sweet pleasure in handling the soft skin. It was exactly what she needed to calm her mental confusion. She had threaded a needle with the European thread Niteesh bought at the fort, when she heard Buck's voice coming from along the river. Her nerves began an erratic dance.

Why was she letting this man affect her so strongly?

~

BUCK SAW Sophia sitting with Niteesh, her head bent over a sewing project. His heart hammered a response. He hadn't expected to see her there. He'd gone hunting with Niteesh's husband, Tarek, in the hopes of driving away the way his arms ached to hold both Sophia and Maxie close—solely to protect them and keep them safe. Or so he tried to convince himself. But his heart longed for something more. Something she signified—home and family.

Having learned how much it hurt to lose Edie and have his dreams die, he meant to deny himself the hope of reviving them.

Seeing Sophia and Maxie so unexpectedly triggered the feelings he struggled to bury.

Sophia glanced his way and looked as startled as he felt. Did he see a flare of welcome before she turned away?

It didn't matter if he did or not. His only concern was keeping them safe out of respect for his friendship with Maximillian.

Little Maxie saw him and toddled over as fast as his short legs would carry him. He stumbled on a bit of sod, but he didn't cry. He scrambled to his feet and rushed to Buck.

Buck lifted him up and held him so they were face to face. From his first glimpse of the baby he'd known he was Maximillian's son. The same dark hair, the same dark eyes, the same full lips. But the look of determination was all Sophia. He shifted Maxie to one arm. The little boy pressed his face to Buck's shoulder in a loving gesture.

Buck's heart filled with an unfamiliar feeling that he couldn't identify, but if he had to, he would say it was affection so strong it pushed aside every other feeling.

Sophia kept her head turned down, as if focusing on the garment on her lap, but her hands were idle.

He lowered himself to the ground beside her. "What are you making?"

She cleared her throat. "A shirt for Maxie." She held up the pieces she had started to stitch together. "Niteesh gave me the doeskin. Isn't it lovely?" She looked across at the other woman. "Thank you."

Niteesh smiled and nodded as she prepared tea for Buck and Tarek. Tarek hung the quail they'd shot beside the tent then sat across from Buck.

Niteesh handed the cups of tea around and gave the two children hard biscuits to chew on.

Tarek studied Sophia and then shifted his gaze to Buck.

Buck met his friend's look with what he hoped would appear as indifference.

Tarek's expression never changed, but Buck saw his smile in his eyes. "She is strong woman. Good woman for Buck."

Buck managed to keep from reacting. Beside him, Sophia's head jerked up and she looked at Tarek.

Buck stared straight ahead as Sophia's gaze came to him and burned a trail along his jaw. He would not move. He would not let anyone guess how the words had startled him, revealing a truth he tried so hard to ignore.

He liked Sophia's determination and strength. She was the kind of woman who would face whatever life threw at her and come out fighting. He liked that in a woman.

Had liked it in Edie, he reminded himself, and look what had happened to her. The last thing he needed in his life was the complication of a headstrong woman.

Sophia turned back to the couple across from them. "I am not his woman."

Niteesh smiled. Tarek nodded. They did not take her words seriously.

"She is not my woman," Buck echoed, even though he knew they would choose to believe whatever they wanted.

He set Maxie beside Sophia, ignoring the child's protests. He pushed to his feet. "I have wagons to take care of." He strode away as if he needed to take care of urgent business and didn't slow down until he reached his circle of wagons. Of course they weren't his wagons. They belonged to those he'd guided from Independence. Luke, Warren, and Judith were involved in an animated discussion. Mary Mae and Donna Grace added their comments.

His guide, Gil, saw him and joined him. "The ladies are planning a traditional Christmas dinner. Judith and her brothers have different customs than Mary Mae and Donna Grace. I'm not sure how they are going to resolve the matter." He leaned against the back of the wagon, next to Buck. "I've decided to stay out of the discussion and let them figure it out themselves."

Buck observed the others. "I remember roast goose and dressing. I'd think the best they could do would be roast venison."

Gil didn't look at Buck but Buck felt his study.

"Are you getting restless to be on your way somewhere?"

He understood Gil's question. Buck didn't care to hang about in one place long. If he wasn't guiding a wagon train, he would often be out hunting or even just exploring. It surprised him to realize he hadn't felt the urge to leave. "I'll stick around and see how the Christmas celebrations go." He hadn't been part of Christmas since the last one he shared with Edie before they left their home to prepare for the trip to Oregon. He didn't recall Christmas being much of an event any time he'd been at Bent's Fort that time of year. The difference this year was Polly's excitement and determination to have a Christmas to remember.

"It is kind of exciting to think of celebrating the season in a special way," Gil said. "Especially with children to share it with." Gil's adopted daughter, Anna, played at Donna Grace's feet.

Buck wished he could deny the pang of longing that swept through him. Luke, Warren, and Gil had been back and forth on the Santa Fe Trail with Buck many times. They were all married now, with children. He, alone, remained single.

He thought of Sophia and Maxie. Something deep inside laid a silent claim to them. Utter nonsense. He pushed away from the wagon. "I've got things to do." He strode away, realized he headed into the open plain, shifted direction and aimed for the fort.

He checked all the animals in the corral then returned to the courtyard.

Sophia entered the gate, Maxie in her arms.

Now that he could see them, his restlessness ended.

She noticed him watching her and drew to a stop. Her gaze held his, drew him like a thirsty horse to water. Slowly, he crossed the yard.

"How is the shirt coming along?"

"Good."

He took Maxie. "He will be one handsome lad in it."

She smiled. "He's handsome without it."

"That he is." They laughed together.

He didn't remember moving but somehow they reached the portico and sat side by side on one of the benches, Maxie contentedly in his arms.

They didn't speak. He felt no need for words. Her presence at his side was all he needed. People moved about in the open square. Some traders went into the trade room. One of the Mexican children chased a ball along one side of the square. All peaceful activities that echoed the feelings inside him: life was pretty good at the moment.

The women who had been by the wagon train earlier entered with their children, still in deep discussion.

"They're planning a Christmas dinner," Buck murmured.

"Polly will be pleased." Sophia chuckled softly. "It seems the child can't get enough of Christmas."

"Let's hope it makes up for all the hard things she's had to deal with."

"Can anything make up for losses?"

He shifted to look into her face. "It must have been hard to lose Maximillian."

She lifted one shoulder in a half dismissive gesture. "I shouldn't have expected it to last forever. Or even to be good."

"Why not? Don't you deserve good things?" He thought she deserved the best.

She considered him for a moment, her eyes filled with the green of a pine tree. Then she blinked. "I think if my own father didn't care enough to hang around, I shouldn't be surprised if no other man does."

Denial rose within him. He couldn't imagine leaving her if they were married, which, of course, they weren't, nor would they be. "Maximillian died. That's not the same as purposely leaving you."

"He left me in most ways long before he died."

She might have thought she hid her hurt, but he saw it in her eyes. Felt it inside his chest like someone had slashed his heart with a knife. Not that he was surprised. He knew what Maximillian was like. It had been his reason for warning him not to marry Sophia. But now that he was growing to see the kind of woman she was, it amazed him that Maximillian hadn't gladly changed to become the sort of husband she deserved.

"I'm sorry." Words were so inadequate. If they'd been in private he would have pulled her to his chest and held her until all her pain disappeared. He had to settle for squeezing her hand, pleasantly surprised when she turned her palm to his and gripped hard. He gladly offered her his strength.

The tense lines framing her eyes faded and a smile touched her lips. "Is this part of your promise to protect me?"

His mouth widened into a smile. "I suppose so." He would gladly shield her from harm and hurt, from pain and disappointment. But a portion of his brain protested.

If he let himself care too much, who would keep him from pain and disappointment?

5

Sophia forced herself to release Buck's hand. She shouldn't have said what she did about her father. It made her sound weak and needy. But when Buck offered his hand, she couldn't resist hanging on.

"I need to see to the wagons and stock." He shifted Maxie to the bench beside her and hurried away.

She could finally breathe without a hitch in her chest. Without her heart tumbling over and over as if rolling down a steep hill.

Mary Mae, Donna Grace, and Judith angled her direction, all of them talking at once.

"We're having a special Christmas dinner."

"Just for us. You know, those of us who came in on Buck's wagon train."

"We've all become family, as much from traveling together as by our marriages."

Sophia knew that excluded her and tried not to mind. They made their way to the dining room for the noon meal. Buck did not join those eating there. Again, she tried not to mind. She ate without saying more than a word or two as the others chattered about their plans, and once the meal was over, she hurried to her room for Maxie to have a nap.

As soon as he fell asleep, she began work on the little shirt. Again, tears clouded her eyes and she was forced to set her sewing aside. Why did her heart yearn for things she couldn't have?

She had never known her father and that left an ache inside. Maximillian had not loved her as she needed, and another bleeding wound had been dealt to her heart. His parents' rejection and then threat to Maxie hollowed out more of her heart.

And she missed her mama.

Mama had given her a small Bible upon her marriage to Maximillian… only the New Testament which meant it was small enough she'd been able to carry it with her. She'd read parts of it in the past and now she pulled it from her travel bag and opened it. She caressed the cover.

"Oh, Mama, what would you advise me to do?"

Words said often filled her mind. *Trust God. Turn to Him and ask His help. Never let the actions of others dictate how you act or even how you feel.*

Sophia hadn't done any of those things. "I'm sorry, Mama." She wiped her eyes and opened the Bible. Mama had told Sophia how she had found her faith through reading the Gospel of John so Sophia turned to that passage and began to read. She read and read, drinking in the Word like a parched land drinks in refreshing rain. Finally, her heart bursting with assurance, she looked up. She knew a God who loved, who saw all needs, who provided. She could trust Him to take care of her.

Why had she not sought this comfort before?

She couldn't wait to share this precious knowledge with Buck and she didn't even try to analyze why she should be so eager to do so.

Maxie wakened and she took him down the steps. Judith and Donna Grace also left their rooms, their babies likewise refreshed from a nap.

Sophia let Maxie play with the other children and sat working on his new shirt as the other ladies discussed their plans for the special Christmas dinner.

At least she would have this garment to give to Maxie.

She lifted the garment. Something wasn't quite right with the sleeve. She wondered if she had made a mistake cutting it or if there was a special way to make it fit. But rather than ask her friends and distract them from their conversation, she folded the soft skin, tucked into her skirt pocket, and picked up Maxie.

Mary Mae looked up. "Are you going somewhere?"

"To see Niteesh." She had told her friend about the Indian woman. "I need her to show me how to make the doeskin shape into the sleeve."

Mary Mae nodded and Sophia made her way to the gate. Outside, she stopped to look about, making sure no more strangers had joined those outside the gate and wondering if she would see Buck. Perhaps he had gone hunting again.

She turned to the right. It wasn't as if she needed him guarding her. Unless newcomers arrived, everyone in and around the fort was known to Buck.

Niteesh saw her approach and hurried out to greet her. "You have tea?"

"I'd love to." She set Maxie on his feet to play with Lola.

"Your man with my man," Niteesh said.

"He's not my man." Sophia knew there was little

point in arguing with Niteesh. She would believe what she wanted to believe. Still, she had to make it as clear as she could.

They drank tea and laughed at their children.

After a bit, Sophia withdrew the shirt from her pocket and held it up. "Why does this sleeve not fit properly?"

Niteesh took the garment, nodding as she examined it. She pulled out a few stitches and pulled the top of the sleeve over her fingers, stretching the soft leather into a curve. She handed it back to Sophia.

"Now it fit."

"Perfect. Thank you."

Niteesh got to her feet. "You and Maxie come with me." She picked up Lola.

Curious, Sophia picked up Maxie and went with Niteesh toward the river. Some horses grazed on the dry grass. They reached scraggly, thick bushes and Niteesh lead along a little path until they reached the river. The water curved away in a wide arc and Niteesh continued that direction.

They rounded the curve and Sophia stopped. Ahead, Buck sat by the edge of the river, fishing.

Why was Niteesh taking her here? They stopped a few feet from Buck. Maxie begged to get down. Sophia released him and he ran to Buck who laughed and took him in his arms.

Niteesh put Lola on the ground and she sidled up to Buck, shy but wanting the attention of this big man.

Buck propped his fishing rod against a rock and pulled the little girl to his knee, smiling from one child to the other.

Sophia blinked hard. What was wrong with her that tears were so close to the surface the last day?

Niteesh found two fishing rods among the bushes. "I bring earlier," she said, as she handed one to Sophia.

"I've never fished."

"Just hang hook in water." Niteesh did that, looking as relaxed as if she was having a nap. She looked at Sophia. "Sit. Fish."

Sophia laughed and sat down, just inches from Buck. Because, she excused herself, she must keep an eye on Maxie. She let her line dangle in the water. If this was fishing, it wasn't half bad.

Niteesh flicked her line and brought up a fish.

Sophia squinted at her line, jiggled it up and down, and then raised it out of the water to stare at the hook. "How'd she do that?" she grumbled.

Buck laughed. "Could be practice?" He waited a moment and added, "And patience?"

She narrowed her eyes at him.

He did his best to look innocent but his eyes twinkled and gave away his amusement.

She laughed. "And I have neither." She lowered her line into the water and sat back. After a moment, she sighed loud and long.

"It sounds like you've used up all your patience."

She nodded, grinning. "I seem to have a very short supply."

Lola crawled from Buck's lap and went to her mother. Maxie shifted, claiming more of Buck for himself.

Sophia smiled but it, too, lived a short life. Why was she letting Maxie get used to Buck's attention? Far too soon she would leave, perhaps go with the others to California, and Buck would continue to go back and forth on the Santa Fe Trail. Remembering the comfort and strength she had experienced reading the Bible, she asked, "Do you have a Bible?"

He looked at the water, adjusted his fishing rod before he answered. "I did have. I suppose it is with the things I left behind after Edie died. I can't rightly say where any of those things are now. Why?"

"My mama gave me a little New Testament and I read some of it today. It was good."

"In what way?" He shifted Maxie to the side so he could look at her more closely.

"I felt so encouraged—maybe that isn't the right word." She shrugged. "I don't know if I can describe it. But reading about how God made all things, about there being life and light in Him, about His grace and the way He showed Himself to mankind... somehow it just made me feel like I could trust Him." It sounded feeble as she tried to put her thoughts into words and yet it had meant so much. She kept her eyes on the fishing line, not wanting to see a reaction from Buck that would minimize her feelings.

He began to speak, his words so soft she strained to hear him. "I haven't thought much about trusting God since Edie died. I worried more about obeying Him in the hopes He would then keep bad things from happening." He gave a mirthless laugh. "Guess I hoped if a person obeyed all the rules—both man's and God's—that no ill would befall them." He drew in a breath and paused.

She waited, letting him take all the time he needed to sort his thoughts.

"I've seen over and over that bad things happen to good and bad people alike. I've seen those same things drive some people to bitterness and others to worship. Can't say as it makes sense and I've come to the conclusion that God is the same always and it's us that chooses which way to go—to be bitter or better."

His words warmed her heart. And amused her too. "Bitter or better. I like that."

They grinned at each other.

"I think I'll try and be better, with God's help," she said.

"Me, too. Maybe I'll see if I can find a Bible to read."

"I could bring mine and we could read it together." Her cheeks warmed at her offer. It sounded far too intimate to think of them sitting together to read the pages of her Bible. And yet, at the same time, it sounded sweet and comforting.

"I'd like that."

She leaned forward. "Where's Niteesh?"

Buck stared at the emptiness beside him. "She must have left. I didn't even notice."

"Nor did I." Had Niteesh purposely left them? She probably had, seeing as she considered Buck Sophia's man. Her cheeks burned. By rights she should return to the fort. But she hadn't caught a fish yet.

They sat side by side, Maxie contentedly playing on Buck's lap. They talked about their families. She learned his parents lived at Big Creek, Ohio where they had a farm and that he had an older brother, Hank, who farmed with them.

"There wasn't enough land for all of us and Edie was eager to head west."

"Is that what you wanted?" she asked.

"I've never regretted leaving. This country has become my home."

She guessed he meant the country between Independence and Santa Fe.

"The others are going to California to start a new life. I'm thinking I might go with them." A beat of silence. "Do you ever think about settling down?" Why had she asked such a question? She hoped he didn't read more into it than simple curiosity. Told herself she wouldn't either.

"I haven't for some time but I have to confess that listening to their plans makes me remember my own dreams of long ago."

"What did those dreams look like?"

His gaze came to her, filled with both hope and despair. "There was a time I wanted nothing more than a home of my own shared with a woman I loved and our children. Sadly, that time has passed."

She couldn't tear herself from his look. And had to resist asking him, *What now? What is your dream now?*

"What about you?" he asked. "What do your dreams look like?"

"That's easy. I simply want someone whom I can trust to always want me. Someone who won't change his mind when things get difficult." She'd spoken without thinking. "At least, that's the dream I once had." She stared at the river.

"I've got a fish."

He pulled out three in rapid succession.

Maxie laughed, bouncing up and down each time Buck caught a fish.

The excitement the two shared sent Sophia into gales of laughter that left her weak inside, but also feeling refreshed and cleansed.

And then her line tightened. She squealed. "Is it a fish?"

"Yes. Pull it out."

"I don't know how."

Buck set Maxie on the ground and came to Sophia. He knelt behind her. "Just like this." He guided her hands.

With his help, she landed her first fish and she laughed. But she couldn't say if it was from the excitement of catching a fish or something more. Something she must deny.

He was staying on the Santa Fe Trail.

She was going to settle down and make a home for Maxie. California sounded better all the time.

"It's time to go back," Buck said.

She couldn't say if he wanted to return because the afternoon had slipped away or if he wanted to end their time together. She wanted the latter.

And if her heart argued otherwise, why would she listen?

~

BUCK CARRIED the fish and Maxie. Sophia took the fishing rods as they made their way back to Niteesh and Tarek's tent. He'd never wanted an afternoon to last forever like he did this one. Talking to Sophia with Maxie playing on his knee, and then having his arms around Sophia, breathing in the sweet scent of her and feeling her hair tickle his chin had filled him with such longings. His feelings for this woman alarmed him. He didn't want to care again and yet he did. So fiercely he would have fought off wild animals with his bare hands to protect her. But he'd learned the folly of thinking he could protect anyone.

Something she said rang through his head. She was going to trust God. But she couldn't trust a man. And she was right to be cautious about her trust. He was afraid he would fail her.

His thoughts still swirled when they arrived back at Niteesh and Tarek's tent. The pair watched them with knowing eyes. If only they would believe him when he said Sophia was not his woman.

If only he didn't wish it was possible.

He wanted to thump himself on his forehead at his wayward thoughts.

He presented his friends with the fish, left the fishing rods, and escorted Sophia back to the fort. At the gate he paused and spoke to the man standing guard.

"Any newcomers?"

"Nope."

Good. That meant he could leave Sophia knowing she'd be safe. He handed Maxie to her. "I'll be back later. If anyone comes, go to your room until I get back."

"I'll be fine. You go do what you have to do." She smiled, though he wondered if it was a little forced. Perhaps she'd found the afternoon as unsettling as he.

"Until later." He touched the brim of his hat and hurried away to do what he needed to do, except he couldn't think what it was. With nothing else to occupy his time, he headed toward the wagons.

Gil, Warren, and Luke were there. Just like old times, but not for much longer. The way they bent their heads together and looked at a map, he knew they were planning their trip already.

They looked up at his approach and straightened.

"Any idea what day it is?" Gil asked.

With a start, Buck realized he didn't. And he always kept track of the days. It was part of his job. He was failing in his responsibilities and he couldn't even regret it. After all, everyone was safe at the fort. So what if he'd allowed himself to enjoy a few days in Sophia's company? Despite his repeated warnings to guard his heart, he wouldn't give back those few days.

"Can't say as I do," he answered.

"Tomorrow is Christmas Eve." Warren looked like he expected Buck to know that.

"I suppose it is." He checked the spokes on the nearest wheel.

Warren continued. "Polly expects us to celebrate so the ladies have planned a Christmas Eve meal for the wagon train folk."

"That's a nice idea." He could see nothing wrong with the wheel and proceeded to check the canvas. Now would be a good time to mend any tears.

"That includes you."

He slowly straightened and faced three men, men who had been his companions for several years. "I think this is a time for families."

"Buck," Luke said. "You are as much a part of our family as anyone else here. It wouldn't be right for you not to be part of our celebration."

The others nodded.

"Reverend and Mrs. Shepton will be joining us," Luke added for good measure.

Warren spoke. "It pains me to think this is our last trip together. We've been talking. We'd like you to come with us to California. You can be our wagon master."

California. Hadn't Sophia said she might be going? What did that matter?

"I suppose I can come to the dinner." It would get him away from the fort. He'd ask one of the men to keep an eye on Sophia if anyone new came. He would have asked Frenchie but the man had gone hunting with a friend.

Even as he made plans, he fought an inner battle. He wanted to be the one to take care of Sophia.

Luke, Warren, and Gil returned to fort, and their wives and children.

Buck stayed and ate with the teamsters. From where he sat he could see if any strangers entered the fort and ensure Sophia and Maxie's safety, yet without being so close that he forgot about never again opening his heart to caring.

He slipped into the fort later, hoping Sophia would have gone to her room. He looked around, didn't see her, and sat on the bench across the courtyard that faced her room. Was she okay? Had she wondered why he had not shown up after their outing? Would she be hurt by his absence?

Ahh. His stomach muscles clenched in reaction to the thought he might have hurt her.

But what choice did he have?

6

The next morning, Sophia rose from her bed, her whole body feeling heavy. Buck had made it clear that he didn't feel any of the same things she had as they sat by the river. Not that she should be surprised. He knew, as did she, that their lives were headed in different directions.

She had to keep her emotions and dreams under control.

As she joined the others for breakfast, she told herself not to look around for Buck, but her gaze searched the room of its own accord. He wasn't there. And hadn't he promised to make sure she was safe? She knew better than to trust his word—any man's word.

"Remember it's Christmas Eve and we'll be having a special dinner," Mary Mae said.

Sophia didn't know if that was an invitation or not. "I'm sure you'll enjoy it."

"But you're coming too." Mary Mae seemed shocked that Sophia would think otherwise.

"I don't know that I should. I wasn't part of the wagon train."

"Nonsense. I insist."

Sophia considered her options. It would help pass the time and even though Maxie was so young, she wanted him to enjoy the season. "Are we exchanging gifts?"

Mary Mae gave a merry chuckle. "According to Polly this is to celebrate Christ's birth. Gifts are exchanged January sixth to commemorate the Three Magi's visit."

"Good, because I haven't finished Maxie's shirt. I better get at it." She let Maxie join the other children at play in the square and sat in the sunshine working on the shirt.

Where was Buck? Had he gone to see Niteesh and Tarek? Or perhaps gone hunting? She thought of the bears and cougars, the men who wouldn't hesitate to harm someone. Was he safe? Maybe he was as close as the wagons that he had guided from Independence.

Would he be at the dinner planned for tonight?

She jolted so hard she jabbed her finger and had to stop sewing until it quit bleeding. Somehow she must excuse herself from the gathering.

But when she spoke to Mary Mae her friend wouldn't hear of it.

"You must come and celebrate with us. I remember the fun we had back in Santa Fe when our parents let us share meals. I've missed that. I've missed you."

There seemed nothing Sophia could say after those words that wouldn't hurt Mary Mae.

Later that day, still feeling caught between her friendship with Mary Mae and the tension she felt at wondering if Buck would be there, she followed her friends to the wagons circled outside the fort.

She glanced around and her breath whooshed out. Buck wasn't there. She wouldn't admit her relief was laced through and through with disappointment.

Polly hurried to greet them. "Welcome to our Christmas Eve celebration. Please, sit here."

Sophia hadn't realized that the young girl was to act as hostess. "What a nice touch," she murmured to Mary Mae.

"Polly has the whole thing planned out. She even came up with the menu."

They gathered on one side of the fire, the warmth welcome against the gathering cold of the afternoon.

Polly stood before them, quivering with excitement. She glanced to the side as someone approached.

Sophia's heart jolted. Buck. He had come. She stifled her reaction.

He glanced about and saw her.

Maxie saw him and bounced his delight.

Buck chuckled and headed toward them. He sat beside Sophia and took Maxie.

She would have tried to hold her son back, but knew it would have precipitated a tantrum and she saw no point in disrupting the proceedings. She kept her attention on Polly as she spoke.

"Today we are going to celebrate Jesus' birthday. Reverend." She signaled Reverend Shepton forward.

Sophia did her best to concentrate on what the reverend said but kept getting distracted by the way Maxie played with Buck's fingers. Buck had a strong hand. One that would hold little boys through the challenges of life.

She shook her head and forced her thoughts back to the preacher and was immediately caught up in his words describing the love God had for each of them to send His one and only Son. Her heart responded with love. It had to be enough. She must not continue to wish for a man to love her enough to be faithful and true.

The reverend finished and sat down.

Sophia closed her eyes and drank in the knowledge of God's love.

Polly signaled Mary Mae and Donna Grace forward. They sang a beautiful duet.

"Now," Polly said, "we will prepare the meal. Please wait while I take care of it." Solemnly, she marched toward the closest wagon.

Several of the teamsters hurried forward and set out planks on sawhorses to create a table. Food simmered in pots and Dutch ovens and Polly supervised the teamsters lifting the pots to the table.

Buck leaned close to Sophia's ear. "I didn't expect to see you here."

She tamped back the unwelcome feeling his words brought. "Would you have stayed away if you'd known I'd be here?" She shifted so she could watch his eyes. Her mouth grew dry as she saw the longing and wanting in them. And then shutters went up and he revealed nothing.

"I promised to protect you. It's easiest if we're in the same vicinity."

"Of course." Why would she think anything else? And why would she wish for something more?

Thankfully Polly interrupted her mental wrangling. "I would like my new papa, Warren, to ask the blessing."

Warren stood, hugged Polly, and prayed.

Sophia's silent prayer contained more than gratitude for the food. *Please, God, help me be sensible. Help me guard my heart and remember You are the only One whose love I can trust.*

She was on her feet as soon as the Amen was spoken. But she couldn't escape Buck. He carried her son and she must see that the child got fed. They followed the others to the table.

"This is quite a buffet," Buck said.

"I wanted to remember Christmas in Mexico," Polly said, indicating the tamales and other Mexican dishes. "But I also wanted to remember what it was like back in Missouri." She pointed out the roast venison. "I couldn't find a goose though."

"It's lovely," Sophia said, a comment echoed by the others. She filled a plate with enough for both herself and Maxie as Buck waited with her son.

"I'll take him and feed him." Buck set Maxie on the ground and she led him away. They sat facing each other as she gave him food and enjoyed the feast as well.

Buck filled his plate and joined her, sitting cross-legged beside her. "I didn't mean I'm not glad to see you."

She looked about, wishing she had chosen a spot closer to the others, and then realized each family had created a little circle of their own. Any of them would surely have welcomed her but she didn't want to intrude. She tried to think how to respond to Buck's words. Before she could, he spoke again.

"I'm considering going to California with the others." His news sent a thrill through her that she quickly quenched. His reasons had nothing to do with her.

"You're thinking of settling down?" She held her breath, waiting for his answer.

"I've always wanted some land of my own."

And a home and family, if she remembered correctly, and knew she did. Would he find someone to love in California?

Neither of them spoke. She couldn't say his reasons for the silence, but the words she wished to say must be kept in her heart. She wanted a home and family too. Most of all she wanted a man who would always return to her with open arms.

He took their empty plates back to the table where the teamsters washed dishes.

When Buck returned, Sophia said, "How did Polly convince those men to be her servants?"

"Everyone is fond of her. And they feel sorry for her. She lost her parents and then her uncle."

"I know. It amazes me how cheerful she is despite it all."

Polly got to her feet and called for their attention. "I want to thank everyone for making this the best Christmas ever. And it's not over." She laughed. "My uncle Sam promised me a special Christmas. He isn't here now." Her words choked off. "But I have a new mama and papa and all these uncles and aunts." She swept her arm to include everyone. "I haven't had such a good Christmas since my first mama and papa were alive."

Sophia knew she wasn't the only one to wipe away a tear.

"Thank you." Polly sat down, and was hugged by Mary Mae and Warren.

The night deepened and the darkness provided Sophia a sense of being alone with Buck, though the flames of the fire revealed the others who seemed to be enjoying quiet time with their family.

Sophia told herself she had no reason to feel alone.

"What was your best Christmas?" Buck asked.

She gave a mirthless chuckle. "Christmas wasn't much different than any other day for us. Mama had to prepare meals for the boarders. About the only thing different was Mama always made a steamed pudding for just the two of us."

Maxie began to nod and she settled him on a blanket by her side and he fell asleep.

"You didn't have a special time with Maximillian?" Buck asked.

She gave a sound of mockery. "I dreaded any special holidays. He grew morose because he couldn't celebrate with his family. He drank more. I lived in fear of what he would do."

He found her hand and squeezed it. "I'm sorry."

"It wasn't your fault."

"I know, but I'm sorry you endured that. That you weren't treated with the kindness and respect you deserve."

His words were like sweet nectar to her wounded soul. Her throat tightened and for a moment she couldn't speak. When she could, she asked, "What Christmas do you remember the fondest?"

He didn't speak for a moment. "I haven't given Christmas much thought for a long time. My parents didn't do anything special, but the Christmas before Edie and I were to be married, she told me how her family celebrated. They shared fond memories of the past year, made funny little cards for each other, and played games Christmas day. She said we would do the same. That would have been my best Christmas only it never happened."

Her heart cracked with sorrow for him and pushing aside every word of warning, she wrapped an arm about his waist and pressed her head to his shoulder. "There will be lots of Christmases ahead when you can do all the things you dreamed of."

He pulled her close. "Seems like this is a good start."

"Polly's Christmas Eve meal?" She asked it in sincerity, but hoped he would have more in mind.

"Polly did a good job, but sharing these few days with you and Maxie are what's made the difference."

She tightened her arm around him. Could she ask for a better Christmas gift than to be given this affirmation? Her greedy heart indeed wished for more but knowing the dangers of remaining in a hug with those dreams and wishes, she eased away.

Donna Grace and Luke picked up their sleeping baby and called, "Goodnight. It's time to tuck this little one into her bed."

Sophia got to her feet. "I need to get Maxie to bed as well." When she bent to pick him up, Buck had already scooped him into his arms, cradling him carefully.

To refuse would disturb the baby so Sophia fell

into step beside Buck as they crossed to the fort. He carried Maxie up the stairs and waited while she opened the door. He stepped inside and gently deposited Maxie on the fur rug. He tucked a blanket about the baby and smiled.

That small gesture and his gentle expression melted Sophia's heart and left her feeling so vulnerable she feared she would either cry or hold her arms out to Buck for a hug.

Thankfully, he went to the door without glancing her way. He stopped and faced her.

"I enjoyed this evening," he said.

"Me too." She narrowed the distance between them. Her excuse being she didn't want to disturb Maxie. "Polly did a wonderful job."

"Yes, she did." He caught her hand and drew her closer. "I think we will all remember this as a special Christmas."

She nodded, studying the button on the front of his coat. "I certainly will think of it with fondness in the future."

He held her chin and tipped her face upward. "Will I be part of that feeling?" His voice was low.

Why was he asking her this? Her eyes went to his. His gaze trailed down her cheeks and lingered on her lips.

She understood he wanted to kiss her, perhaps

waited for her permission, and even though she knew she should step away, she lifted her face to his. After all, it was Christmas Eve and she might as well crown it with something to carry with her into the future.

He caught her lips gently. She tasted the sweetness of the cookies they'd had. Her heart disobeyed her every order and clamored upward, reaching for more, wanting more. Wanting forever.

He broke away. "Good night." He stepped outside and closed the door.

She stared at the slab of wood between them. The kiss was only a goodwill gesture given because of the season.

If only she could believe that.

She sank to the mat beside Maxie. What was she going to do with her wayward heart?

~

BUCK TOOK the stairs in three bounds. His steps didn't slow until he reached the wagons. Several of the teamsters lingered around the glowing coals, talking about the Christmas Eve dinner. They paid him little attention as he got his bedroll and climbed into one of the empty wagons for the night. With no intention of continuing on to Santa Fe, Luke, Warren, and Gil had sold their goods here.

But sleep did not come. Why had he told Sophia that spending the evening with her was a good start to enjoying future Christmases? Even if they both joined the trek to California....

Could he allow himself to once again dream of home and family and a forever love?

Even if he did, would she ever be prepared to trust him, given her past experiences?

He crossed his hands under his head and smiled into the darkness and for tonight—only because it was Christmas Eve—allowed himself to picture watching Maxie grow up, sharing special smiles, and kisses with Sophia.

He woke next morning with his heart full of hope. Today was Christmas. Polly had said they would exchange gifts on January sixth according to the Mexican tradition. That gave him a few days to come up with a perfect gift for Sophia and Maxie. He would get Niteesh to prepare a soft rabbit fur for Sophia and maybe even fashion it into a hat or mittens. For Maxie? He wasn't much of a carver but he could make some blocks of wood for the boy.

Eager to get on with his task he went immediately to the tent of his Indian friends.

Niteesh laughed at his suggestion. "Fine idea for your woman."

"She's not—" He stopped as he realized he wished she was or would be.

His heart too unsettled to face them, he trekked along the river, his thoughts filled with hopes and plans. It was Christmas day. Was there a better time for him to look toward a new future?

7

Sophia glanced continually toward the gate but Buck did not show up. If she needed any other evidence that the kiss they shared last night meant nothing, this was it. Obviously he did not feel the same as she did. When she wakened this morning, she'd risen eagerly, anticipating seeing him, perhaps sharing a quiet walk with him away from the hustle and bustle of the fort.

Not that she was disappointed. Hadn't she learned long ago that the men in her life made plans with little regard for her feelings? Why should she think him any different?

And yet she did. Or rather, had.

Mary Mae noticed Sophia's distraction and frequent glances toward the gate. "He'll come. You can count on Buck. He's one of the most reliable men I know."

Perhaps when it came to taking care of a wagon train. But Sophia kept her thoughts to herself. "I wasn't watching for him."

Mary Mae chuckled. "Of course you weren't."

Thankfully, Polly called Mary Mae away at that moment, so the discussion ended.

Sophia sat on a bench that happened to allow her a view of the gate and worked on Maxie's shirt. Her son played at her feet but fussed often. She wouldn't admit that he seemed to miss Buck.

She should never have let Maxie get fond of him. But didn't he need a man in his life?

Her thoughts drifted, unattended, to the dream she had clung to all her life. A home where a man welcomed her and swung her off her feet in joy at returning home.

It was almost noon when horses clattered through the gate. Newcomers! Her heart slammed into her ribs. Her fear grew as the riders streamed in.

"No." The word burned up her throat. She recognized the man in the midst of the riders. Maximillian's uncle Gilberto. He would be here for one reason only.

She grabbed Maxie and drew back into the overhang of the roof. She couldn't hope to hide forever but so few knew her as Sophia Lorenzo. Maybe if she stayed in her room until the riders left again....

She pulled her shawl over her head and began a slow shuffle toward the nearest set of stairs. How had her life gone from the best Christmas Eve since she was a child to the worst Christmas Day ever?

Where was Buck and his promise to protect her?

She made it to her room and shut the door firmly behind her. Maxie wouldn't like being confined to this small space especially if he heard the other children at play. Mary Mae would surely miss her and come to investigate.

It wasn't long before Maxie began to fuss at the door. Her own stomach rumbled so she knew he was hungry. But she wouldn't leave the room. Gilberto Lorenzo would expect to be welcomed like royalty and be seated with the most important man, but that did not mean he wouldn't be asking questions and expecting answers. He'd be studying every woman in the fort and likely go poking around the wagons outside.

She pulled Maxie from the door and played finger games with him which amused him for a short time. She could only hope Mary Mae came to her rescue.

A short time later, someone rapped on the door and Mary Mae called softly, "It's me."

Sophia opened the door and hid around the wooden frame until Mary Mae entered the room and then closed the door tightly behind her.

"I brought you food. I knew you wouldn't be showing your face with Gilberto Lorenzo snooping around." She handed Sophia two covered dishes. "I said I was taking this to a friend who was indisposed."

Maxie drooled as he saw the food and she fed him first.

"What is he saying?"

"He's asking for you but people are a little cautious because they know you as Greta. Someone did say there was a young woman with a little boy about the age of the child he seeks so he's suspicious. It won't be long before they realize it's you he is asking after."

"I know." She finished feeding Maxie then turned to her own food. "How long can I hide, do you suppose?"

The way Mary Mae rolled her head back and forth did not offer much encouragement.

Sophia choked down the food she'd lifted to her mouth. "Could I hide in one of the wagons?"

"Gilberto is watching the gate closely."

Sophia shuddered. "I will not go back with him. Nor will I let him take Maxie."

"Of course you won't."

"Where is Buck? He promised to help me."

"I haven't seen Buck since last night. Warren said he hasn't either."

"What choice do I have but to hide here as long as I can and hope if they discover my presence, someone will defend me?" Where was Buck and why was she pinning her hopes on him when he had disappeared without so much as a word? "Thank goodness Maxie will sleep a few hours. He's not going to like hiding out here."

"I'll ask Judith to bring Anna to visit later." Mary Mae took the dishes, and slipped out.

Sophia closed the door securely and leaned against it feeling trapped in the safety of the room. She settled Maxie for his nap then paced the floor, her thoughts too tangled for her to settle. She would not give up Maxie without a fight, but the Lorenzos were accustomed to getting what they demanded. Would her friends be able to defend her against Gilberto's plans?

Her footsteps began to stir up dust and she retreated to the bench by the fireplace and opened her Bible to read. She'd decided to trust God, but it was hard when things piled up against her. She calmed herself. What kind of trust was it that wouldn't last through challenges?

She would trust God and give Buck a chance to explain himself.

Judith visited later, bringing tea and cookies. The little ones played on the fur rug and chased each other about. But after a few minutes Maxie leaned against the door and cried.

Her heart went out to him. He couldn't understand why he must be cooped up.

"What is that man doing?" Sophia asked.

Judith studied her. "He's spreading lies."

"Like what?"

"He says you've kidnapped Maxie and that you are a woman of ill repute."

Sophia looked down, unable to meet her friend's gaze.

"No one believes him."

Sophia knew Judith meant to be encouraging, but among all those at the fort, there would be some who would think the words must have some truth to be spoken.

"The men are working at getting you to a safe hiding place."

Sophia's heart lightened. "What are they planning?"

"Somehow they'd have to get the Lorenzo crew

distracted." She lifted a shoulder. "I'm sorry. So far no one has come up with a good plan." She gave a mirthless chuckle. "Luke said maybe we should roll you up in a buffalo hide and carry you out that way."

Sophia shuddered at the idea.

."Gil thought it would attract too much attention."

Judith turned the talk to activities of the other women. No doubt she hoped to distract Sophia from her loneliness but it only made her feel more imprisoned than ever.

After a bit, Anna grew bored and Judith departed with the little girl. "I'll be sure someone brings you supper."

"Buck hasn't shown up?" She had promised herself she wouldn't ask but she had to know.

"Gil says he must have gone hunting."

Sophia leaned against the door after Judith left. Buck picked a fine time to leave. Not that she should let herself think he would take care of her.

She must trust God to help her take care of herself. But she had no idea what she could do with Gilberto guarding the gateway.

∽

BUCK HURRIED BACK to the fort as darkness descended. He had not planned to be gone so long but he'd found an injured trapper and couldn't leave him. He managed to get the man to his meager shack, tended his wounds, made sure he had water, food, and firewood before he left him. On the way back, he'd stopped to ask Tarek to check on him.

All the while, the delay crowded his thoughts. He wanted to be with Sophia, gauge her reaction to the kiss they'd shared last night, and enjoy spending time with her.

Would she have missed him? Or was she happily occupied with her friends? Perhaps making plans for the trip to California. He had made up his mind. He would be joining the others heading that direction.

He hoped Sophia would welcome his presence.

He reached the gate and stopped. A stranger leaned against the corner post watching him.

Did he know this man? Perhaps not, but his haughty bearing sent alarm skidding up and down Buck's arms. He drew closer and swallowed hard. There was no disguising how much the man looked like Maximillian. The Lorenzos had come after Sophia and he had not been there to protect her.

How could he have let other things distract him

from his promise? How could he ever hope she would trust him when he'd failed already?

"You there," the man called.

Buck stopped, taking a casual stance with his legs wide and his arms crossed. "You talking to me?"

"Yes, you. Who are you?"

Buck didn't care for the man's tone. "Who wants to know?"

"I am Gilberto Lorenzo."

Buck shrugged. "Means nothing to me."

The man looked offended but Buck didn't care. "Have you by any chance seen a young woman with a little boy?"

Buck snorted. "Mister, look around you. There must be a dozen young women with small children."

"Mind your tongue."

Buck didn't blink before the other man's hard glare.

Lorenzo continued. "This woman might or might not be calling herself a Lorenzo. The child she has is not hers. He's a Lorenzo heir and I've come to return him to his rightful home."

It was all Buck could do not to react to the lies. "Best of luck finding them, mister." He pushed on by.

The man grabbed his arm.

Buck shook his hand off and gave him his

hardest look. Three men stepped from the shadows. It was easy for Lorenzo to be bossy and controlling when he had others to do his fighting.

"The woman is not what she claims to be. She is a loose woman off the streets and hoping to profit from kidnapping the boy."

Buck's fists curled. His stomach soured. He clenched his teeth until he had control over his emotions. "Mister, those are ugly accusations. There might be those around here who would take objection to hearing them."

"You one of them?"

"One of many, so watch your step." He strode toward the dining room, hoping to find someone to tell him if Sophia and Maxie were safe.

He stepped inside. Before his eyes even adjusted to the light, someone called his name.

"Buck."

The women from the wagon train sat together. He joined them. "Where's Sophia?" Too late, he realized he should have asked about Greta.

Mary Mae answered his question. "She's hiding in her room but that man is beginning to get suspicious. He's also telling lies and I fear someone will believe him."

"Where are the men?"

"They've gone to the wagons. They're trying to

plan a way to get her out of the fort and hide her somewhere."

"There is a way that might work. But I'll need help."

"Anything."

The women leaned close as he described his plan. Then they hurried to carry it out.

He ached to go to Sophia's room and assure her he would take care of her but knew it was best if he waited.

The women returned with their husbands. Judith handed him a Mexican sarape. He traded his cowboy hat for a sombrero.

Judith pulled a heavy shawl about her head and shoulders and wrapped little Anna under the material. Gil put on Buck's coat and hat and they stepped from the dining room.

Buck went through the kitchen and out to the portico where he edged his way toward the closest set of stairs. He waited as Judith and Gil shuffled their way across the courtyard.

Lorenzo stepped from the gateway. "Hold up there." Several men removed from the shadows and circled Gil and Judith.

It was Buck's signal and he raced up the stairs, tapped on the door of Sophia's room and softly called her name.

She opened the door. "Buck. Where have you been?"

"I'll explain later. We must hurry. Put this over your head." He lifted Maxie and wrapped him up, praying the child would be quiet until they escaped. "Follow me."

"Where are we going?"

"Trust me."

She nodded and they slipped from the room.

Below them Gil and Judith were fending off the Lorenzo crew. The others had joined in, making it impossible for Gilberto to get a good look at the pair and the baby in her arms, now crying.

Buck practically dragged Sophia down the stairs and toward the passageway to the corrals. The horses shuffled at their intrusion then ignored them. "There's one gate. Once we're out of here, we'll head for the river and I'll take you to Tarek and Niteesh. They'll hide you." He knew they would take Sophia to another family a distance away to keep her safe.

They made it to the gate and he slipped the latch to release it, then held it for her to follow him out.

"Stop right there." A voice with a thick accent uttered the order. Something that he was certain was a gun jabbed into his back.

He stopped. Tried to think what the best thing to

do was. Tell Sophia to run. Hide. Or keep her at his side. He preferred the latter.

"Don't either of you move." The man's words made up Buck's mind. He only wished he could pull her close and reassure her. But at least he had Maxie.

"I will protect you both no matter what," he whispered.

"Mr. Lorenzo," the man behind them yelled. "I got someone."

By now Lorenzo would know he had the wrong couple cornered in the courtyard.

"Let's go to the gate," the man ordered them and they went that direction, a sharp jab in his back reminding Buck that this was serious business.

They entered through the gate. Lanterns and the light of campfires provided uncertain light. Lorenzo grabbed one of the lanterns and shone it in Sophia's face then yanked the blanket from Maxie and did the same.

Maxie screamed at the rough treatment.

Buck had an incredible urge to push the man to the ground but he tempered his reaction. Whatever he did would affect the outcome of this situation.

"This is the woman I told you about." Lorenzo spoke to the crowd that had swelled to include most of those staying at the fort and perhaps a few of the teamsters who had been attracted by the noise. "This is the woman that stole the Lorenzo child. She's an evil woman."

Buck could take no more. He pulled Sophia to his side, covering her as best he could with his arm. "You tell lies. This is Sophia Lorenzo. She married your nephew who has passed on. She is an honorable woman and good mother and I venture to say everyone in this fort will testify to the truth of my words."

A rumble of assent rose.

"That child is the Lorenzo heir. He belongs with the Lorenzo family."

"No sir. He is Sophia's son and belongs with her." He looked about the gathering, saw only friendly faces apart from Lorenzo's men. "You gathered here have seen her. Can any of you raise a doubt about her suitability as a mother?"

"Nay." The answer came loud and clear, and as a body, those assembled lined up beside Sophia.

Charles Bent had joined them. "Mr. Lorenzo, you have no authority here. We will not tolerate you taking that boy from his mother."

Expectant silence met the man's words and then Lorenzo scowled at them all. "I have my doubts that the child is even a Lorenzo. The woman probably doesn't know who the father is."

He signaled to his men and they stomped from the fort.

Sophia sagged against Buck, crying softly.

He handed Maxie to Mary Mae and led Sophia to a quiet corner. The others hovered nearby, ready to spring to her defense again should the need arise but staying far enough away to allow them some privacy.

He held Sophia and wiped her tears as she cried. "You are safe now. The Lorenzos won't bother you again."

"Those ugly words," she stammered.

"No one believes them." He tipped her tear-stained face up to look at him. "I certainly don't."

She nodded. "I'm glad."

He must make one thing clear. "I'm sorry I wasn't here to protect you as I promised." He explained what had happened.

"But you did protect me as you promised. Thank you."

"Sophia, I would like the right to take care of you the rest of my life."

She wiped the last of her tears from her eyes. "How do you plan to do that?"

"I'd like to marry you."

She blinked. "Why?"

He thought it was obvious. "Because I love you

so much it consumes my every thought. Can you have just a smidgen of love for me?"

She laughed. "Not a smidgen. Nope."

He hoped his face did not reveal his disappointment.

"Buck Williams, I love you a whole lot. With every thought and every moment of my day."

He pulled her to her feet. "Does that mean you'll marry me?"

"It most certainly does."

He kissed her, his lips lingering as he drank in her giving and trusting. He broke off, his heart so full he wanted to shout. Instead, he lifted her from her feet and swung her in a wide arc, delighted when she laughed.

EPILOGUE

"This is it," Polly called to everyone in sight. "This is the day we exchange gifts."

That might be the big excitement for Polly, but for Sophia, it was her wedding day. The last few days had been delightful as she and Buck read her Bible together, prayed, planned the future, and played with Maxie. They'd shared stories of growing up. Sophia talked about her marriage to Maximillian, finding there remained no pain associated with those memories. Buck's love had erased the bad stuff. She knew she could trust him to always treat her right.

When he'd learned that swinging her off her feet was part of a long-cherished dream, he made a practice of doing it often.

He'd expressed one fear—he thought he had failed her in not being there when Maximillian's uncle had come. Over and over, she had assured him that all that mattered was he was there in the end.

"I will never be a helpless female," she'd assured him.

"But you will accept my help?"

"I'd love to."

She smiled at her memories and turned her thoughts to the present. It was time for their wedding.

Mary Mae came to Sophia and brought a mantilla that had belonged to her mother. "We have all worn it for our weddings," she said. She helped put it in place on Sophia's head. They waited in the trade room. Buck and the others had gone into the council room. Sophia had said she would walk to her husband-to-be on her own. Her father had left her years ago but now it didn't matter so much. She knew Buck would not leave her.

Mary Mae left her and an accordion began to play.

Sophia entered the next room, saw Buck waiting, and went to his side.

Reverend Shepton had them exchange vows and

declared them man and wife. Sophia spared a fleeting thought about how nice it was that Reverend Shepton and his wife had decided to join the journey west.

Sophia and Buck kissed for the first time as Mr. and Mrs. Williams.

"I have found a man worthy of my love and trust," she whispered to him.

"And I have found a woman worthy of *my* love and trust."

"Now it's time for the gifts," Polly called. They sat on benches along the wall as Polly passed a gift to each of them. For the ladies, she had hemmed white handkerchiefs. For the men, handkerchiefs in red cotton.

Sophia had finished a shirt for Maxie and Niteesh had helped her make mittens for Buck.

Buck presented Sophia with a beautiful pair of rabbit fur mittens and a set of blocks for Maxie, who immediately sat at Buck's feet to play with them.

Polly looked at the leather-bound journal Mary Mae and Warren had given her. Her gaze circled the room. "This is the best Christmas ever."

Buck wrapped his arm about Sophia. "I have to agree." They kissed and if anyone minded, they didn't say so. In fact, when she glanced up she saw her friends smiling at her.

She knew the future held all her dreams and wishes in the shape of her loving husband.

ALSO BY LINDA FORD

Contemporary Romance

Montana Skies series

Cry of My Heart

Forever in My Heart

Everlasting Love

Inheritance of Love

Historical Romance

Dakota Brides series

Temporary Bride

Abandoned Bride

Second-Chance Bride

Reluctant Bride

War Brides series

Lizzie

Maryelle

Irene

Grace

Made in United States
Troutdale, OR
03/24/2024

18694849R00080